THE SHADOW OF POLVOSE

THE SHADOW OF POLVOSE

When Carla answered an advertisement for a job in Cornwall, requiring an 'adventurous type', she had no idea of the drama and mystery that would surround her when she reached Polvose – an isolated country house near Fowey overlooking the river. Her relationship with her employer, Vanessa Ingram, whose husband Melvin was a strange and difficult man, drew her into a situation both dangerous and romantic, particularly when she met Adrian, the Ingram solicitor. Carla gradually learned the secrets of the Ingrams, and that knowledge finally involved her in murder...

The Shadow of Polvose

by

Sharon Moore

Dales Large Print Books
Long Preston, North Yorkshire,
BD23 4ND, England.

British Library Cataloguing in Publication Data.

Moore, Sharon
    The shadow of Polvose.

    A catalogue record of this book is
    available from the British Library

    ISBN   1-84262-451-2 pbk

First published in Great Britain in 1966 by
Hurst & Blackett Ltd.

The moral right of the author has been asserted

Published in Large Print 2006 by arrangement with
The estate of Sonia Deane, care of Rupert Crew Ltd.

All Rights reserved. No part of this publication may be
reproduced, stored in a retrieval system, or transmitted in any
form or by any means, electronic, mechanical, photocopying,
recording or otherwise without the prior permission of the
Copyright owner.

678241

MORAY DISTRICT COUNCIL
DEPARTMENT OF
LEISURE AND LIBRARIES
F

Dales Large Print is an imprint of Library Magna Books Ltd.

Printed and bound in Great Britain by
T.J. (International) Ltd., Cornwall, PL28 8RW

1

Carla Selby read aloud from the personal column of *The Times*, 'Wanted, intelligent companion with secretarial qualifications. Adventurous type essential. Write Box D, 409.'

'Intriguing,' she commented thoughtfully. 'I think I'll apply.'

Her parents, Lee and Tessa, exchanged understanding glances. Although nothing had been said, they realised that Carla was weary of her present job as secretary to Gordon Knight, a business tycoon, who had no interest in life beyond making money.

'Companion,' Tessa echoed. 'I wonder just what that entails.' She watched Carla carefully as she spoke, familiar with the light of enthusiasm in Carla's expressive grey eyes – enthusiasm which always led to decision, never to a fading interest. She liked that quality in her daughter, finding people who never knew what they wanted both boring and weak. Carla might infuriate, appear to be quite irresponsible on occasions, but she had a basic stability, even a wisdom, not always found in a girl of twenty-two.

'I wonder if it is a job abroad,' Carla

exclaimed. 'Not that I care.'

Her father smiled. 'Only one way to find out. Adventurous type. You'll certainly qualify there!'

Carla looked from face to face. She liked her parents as well as loving them. They had always understood all the things that the parents of her friends failed to do. Her mother was fifty, but looked far younger, her hair still dark and her skin glowing and unlined. Her father, a dentist (as he always said, the most unpopular and unromantic profession on earth), had a quiet charm as though he nursed a secret formula for happiness.

'I shall miss you,' Carla said suddenly. She looked out over the garden which, on that May morning, was full of blossom and sun which seemed to be filtered through the trees in a shower of golden light. Morgan, the gardener, pottered among his roses – a bent, gnarled figure, reminding Carla of an everlasting oak. His skin was a deep mahogany, his face pleated into furrows like the soil he tilled. 'Ascot's been a lovely place in which to grow up, and this old cottage–' She stopped abruptly.

'Neither will disappear in your absence,' her father teased.

'So you think I shall get the job? You always have instincts about things.'

Lee felt a strange pang of fear as he said, 'You'll get it.' He wanted to dissuade her from applying, but adhered to his policy never to interfere, or give advice.

Carla experienced a tingle of excitement. Now she was grateful she had given in her notice to Gordon Knight a month previously, but since he had begged her to reconsider her decision, she had not discussed the matter even with her parents. Without anything particularly attractive appearing, she might have remained for a while longer. But there was just *something* about the words *Adventurous type essential* that demanded more than mere routine efficiency. She had no ties; no man in whom she was interested, even though her escorts were (as Lee humorously put it) 'Like a string of race horses and as numerous as the starters in the Grand National!' In addition, Carla argued, her younger sister, Sarah – although at boarding school – would take the edge off her own departure and keep the cottage overflowing with teenagers.

It was exactly a week later that, having been accepted for the job, Carla set off in her own small car for Cornwall. She had spoken over the telephone to her new employer, Vanessa Ingram, and liked the sound of her voice and attitude generally. At the same time, she found it a little odd that a young married woman should need a companion. Mrs Ingram had volunteered her age as thirty-two and not been deterred by the fact that Carla was ten years her junior. On the other hand, the Ingram house was, apparently, isolated and near Fowey. There had been no evasion on this point, and Carla had made the stipulation that she should bring her own car and be free to use it in the spare time given to her. She knew very little about Cornwall, having been there only once before. This fact added to her enthusiasm.

On the journey down she began to take stock of herself emotionally. She knew that her self-criticism amounted almost to a vice and that she could take herself to pieces as one might pick at a badly knitted garment. What was it she wanted out of life? And from what was she now escaping? The mediocrity of unsatisfying, innocent flirtations. Relationships without depth, or sexual involvement. On the surface she had been reasonably successful and followed through the secretarial training generously given by her father. There was nothing in her home life that jarred and nothing – by way of freedom – she had been denied. She could have taken a flat in London with many of her friends and been far more tied than she had been at Ascot. Yet, here she was, driving down to Cornwall into the unknown. Some instinct warned her that she was going from light into shadow. What sense did that make? And in that second of analysis, she found her answer. She wanted a secure emotional background with someone she could love.

Colour mounted her cheeks, because the ideal seemed so ordinary. For all that, she knew she was escaping from the happy parties, the laughter, the boredom of immature men. It was not that she disliked gaiety; on the contrary, she loved it, but she wanted to find something that gave it depth and meaning. In realising that she had never known unhappiness, she appreciated, also, that she had never known happiness at any level of personal fulfilment. She was escaping to see if, in whatever adventure lay ahead, there was a purpose rather than a facile acceptance of tinsel-garnished emptiness. She had not violated the example set by her parents, but their marriage had already reached its harbour, while she knew that she must find a turbulent sea. That sounded dramatic, she told herself fiercely and with a certain disgust, but she knew that self-deception was the worst form of dishonesty and could serve no good purpose. It struck her that the word, tragedy, could be a misnomer, for never to know even the brush of its dark shadow might mean that the greatness dormant within the soul might be lost in triviality. Suddenly her thoughts, her reflections, made her free. Quietude revealed some intimate part of her character which, previously, had been elusive.

The countryside rushed by. The rolling downs of Wiltshire, the panoramic views of

Somerset and Devon. She stopped for a hurried buffet meal at Exeter, before reaching Cornwall. There, the mood changed and she felt the fascination of its strange influence, almost as though it had detached itself from England and created a world, a personality, of its own. As time passed, she was to learn that Cornwall had to be discovered, rather than seen. It was not a shop putting all its wares in the window; it was a treasure hunt.

She reached Fowey just after four o'clock and felt that she had turned back to one of her childhood stories and found Toy Town. Even her Mini-Minor seemed too large for its narrow streets, where pedestrians had to lean back against the walls of houses to allow a car to pass. She had no time to appreciate the harbour, or the yachts at anchor, because she had lost her way and the crudely drawn map, sent to her by Vanessa Ingram, was not very helpful. She stopped and hailed a rugged-faced Cornishman who smelt of the sea. He studied her with a polite criticism and said disconcertingly, 'I see'd un comin' up along. Where be to?'

Carla tried to explain. 'Polvose – the Ingram house.'

His expression darkened. 'Ingram! Ah, that be in woods, near creek.' There was no sympathy in his voice as he added, 'Trespassers – they be forbid.'

Carla convinced him that she was not a trespasser and he gave her a reasonable description of how to get there, mentioning Lanteglos Church and adding, a trifle tartly, that the Hall Walk would be simpler. It was quite obvious that he disliked cars, but, as she was about to drive off, he grinned. 'Good luck to ee.' Then glancing up at the dark threatening skies, he added, 'There be a proper storm comin' up.'

Carla laughed. 'I love storms ... thank you.'

He was right. A *proper* storm broke almost as Carla left him. Day suddenly became night as the lightning cut through the sinister darkness, illuminating it with flashes of flame and blue. Thunder crackled like machine-gun fire against a wartime barrage. Carla had to switch on the headlights in order to complete the last tortuous part of the journey which seemed like climbing Everest. A weird eerie sensation crept over her as she suddenly saw a signpost marked Polvose. And as she drove along the narrow winding drive, she had glimpses of a magnificent view of the waters of the creek far below.

At last, she saw the house. Her first impression was of looking at an abstract painting of tragedy. It stood in the shadow of the storm, its square, granite walls glistening as the rain washed over them. The large windows were set back and peered like the eyes of an old man from a weather-beaten face. The grounds were extensive and lost themselves in woodland. An orchard quivered and shuddered as the storm raged over it, mocking the feeble struggle of the frail blossoms on the trees, as they tried to cling to the branches which had given them life. Now the wind was whining and howling as though every force of nature was determined to reach a final point of destruction. Carla braked at the front door – mentally and physically exhausted. She had sought adventure, she told herself. Here it was!

At that second, as she switched off the engine of the car, a slim delicate figure appeared beneath the portico. Her voice did battle with the noise as she called, 'Carla Selby?'

Carla slid out of the driving seat and dashed for cover. She smiled. 'Yes ... Mrs Ingram?'

Her employer nodded. 'I've been so worried about your driving through this ghastly storm.'

'I prefer to be certain of my way when it is as dark as this,' Carla admitted.

'I'm not very good at giving directions, or drawing maps, I'm afraid. But you are here and that is such a relief.'

Vanessa Ingram tried, to the best of her ability, to take stock of the girl entering her house. She knew that if any element of

14

doubt, or disharmony, should intrude, everything on which she had counted would be lost. Carla's good-tempered attitude, her grin of amusement, countered any fears.

'Leave everything in the car. Wells will attend to it all. He and his wife look after things here.' A wistful note crept into Vanessa Ingram's voice. 'I almost inherited them from my parents when they died.'

In turn, Carla tried to assess Vanessa Ingram as they went into the house. There was a sadness about her, which even her warm smile did not remove. It was a smile painted on her lips, but not reflected in her eyes. A Nordic fairness of skin and hair created the illusion that she was not English – an erroneous illusion. She led the way into a large hall which was dominated by a chimney corner and beamed fireplace. Flowers, beautifully arranged, stood beneath a vast window which went from the ground floor to the second. Highly polished copper, brass, lantern-type lamps illuminated the scene, throwing shadows over the dark panelled walls. Outside, the storm still raged, its temper not yet spent.

Then suddenly, silently, Mrs Wells appeared. She was a gaunt woman, squarely built, whose discreet black dress hung on her shapelessly. There was distrust and suspicion in her beady brown eyes as they met Carla's with an expression which, if interpreted, demanded to know what right she had to be there. She took over and showed Carla to her room.

'I hope you will find everything to your liking,' she said, indicating the large divan bed and the general colour scheme of the surroundings which shaded to pale apple green and faint pink. She made a gesture towards a door which led to an adjoining bathroom.

'It is very beautiful,' Carla said appreciatively.

'Everything is beautiful in this house.' Mrs Wells spoke in a tone which left nothing more to be said and, as she finished the sentence, she walked to one of the vast windows and, before drawing the curtains, pointed to the scene below where a turbulent sea lashed itself into the mood of the storm. 'Be careful of this window,' she warned. 'Never open it too wide. Someone was killed through leaning out too far.' She moved away. 'Tea will be ready in a quarter of an hour.'

Alone, Carla just stood and stared. It was like going back into another century. Here was isolation, she decided, added to which was a way of life her own generation had not known. It struck her that Mrs Wells was a woman of tenacity who could, very subtly, rule the household. It would not be wise to cross swords with her.

Vanessa Ingram appeared at the doorway, just as Carla was ready to go downstairs. Her approach was timid and gentle as she inquired if everything was in order, adding a little breathlessly, 'Mrs Wells is so good, I hate to interfere with the way she runs things.' There was a nervous note in her voice as she added, 'The storm has stopped, thank heaven.'

Carla had not noticed; she had unpacked, taken care of her make-up, even plunged into the bath for a matter of minutes and was refreshed and interested in absorbing all that was going on around her. *Adventurous type essential.* Something told her that the words were not a misnomer. She wondered exactly where Mr Ingram fitted into this picture.

Over the tea cups, Vanessa Ingram told her. Melvin Ingram was a director of a firm of electronics. Trying to relate the facts to the individual, she gathered that he was a brilliant man, whose mind was a vast computer which craved only the food of knowledge – statistics – to maintain perfection.

'You see,' Vanessa Ingram said with a childish acceptance, 'my husband is away a very great deal and it is very lonely here.' She smiled apologetically. 'That must make me sound very weak.'

Carla knew that the right answer was vital and she said honestly, 'One can love a place

– a house – but being in it alone can mean desolation. I have never been able to understand why so few people realise that real loneliness is an emotional thing and not a matter of meeting dozens of people, or going to parties.'

Vanessa Ingram said tensely, 'It can also be a lack of communication between two people.'

Carla felt the cold breath of fear; the sinister realisation that she had walked into tragedy. Everything around her shouted the word, because of the juxtaposition of obvious success against the deep chasm of emptiness. She tried to relieve the grey mood by saying, 'This would be the most wonderful place in which eventually to achieve communication.'

'Unfortunately temperaments are not changed by places, or the beauty of surroundings.' The words came slowly as though each one hurt.

Something strong and determined in Carla's character forced her to say firmly and directly, 'Mrs Ingram, in your advertisement you said "Adventurous type essential." Just what did you mean by that? Quite frankly I have no wish to be involved in any unhappy marriage. There would be no point in my remaining unless you give me your definition of adventurous.'

Carla never forgot the deathly silence that followed. It was as though every clock had stopped, every breath of air had been sucked from the room. Then the answer came like the thunder which had died down. The woman opposite her appeared to crumple like a concertina. She put her hands over her face to hide the tears which, otherwise, would have fallen down her cheeks. Her voice was choking, her words just audible, *'I wanted you here because I know that my husband is going to murder me.'* She added pitifully, 'I just could not face it alone.'

Carla shivered; the atmosphere was terrifying and yet, in some uncanny way, fascinating. She said, trying to sound disbelieving, 'Isn't that rather a fantastic statement?'

Vanessa Ingram, calm now, shook her head. 'I can understand your reaction, but you wanted the truth to which you are entitled.' She looked suddenly hopeless. 'I felt I could trust you the moment I heard your voice over the telephone and I like your directness.'

Carla asked: 'Does anyone else know of this? Or your fears?'

'No one. It would be impossible if I were to betray my feelings – my *instinct*. My husband is a strange man, but I'm still in love with him,' she added simply. 'He can be so kind and charming and equally sadistic.' She held Carla's gaze, 'I'm not mad, or suffering from any delusions. I can face up to most things, but his anger destroys me. That's where I'm weak.'

19

'But you must have something stronger than instinct to justify your belief.' Carla made a gesture to convey reassurance. 'No one—'

'No one can be expected to take me seriously. I suppose I just prayed you might be the exception.'

'I am.' Carla's skin seemed to lift from her flesh. She had wanted adventure. But *murder* was another matter. Was the woman sitting opposite her normal? There was nothing to indicate anything to the contrary. But the mind was unfathomable and the maze of its thoughts like dark tributaries spreading from a larger, wind-whipped river. On the face of it every word, every expression, was suggestive of truth. The poignant utterance, 'I'm still in love with him,' told a story which Carla sensed to be dramatic as well as tragic.

Vanessa Ingram leaned forward and there was a desperate urgency about her as she pleaded, 'Oh, please stay; please stay. Having you here may change it all. Ease the tension.'

There was something child-like about the remarks, as though a fugitive hope lay concealed in them. Self-preservation urged Carla to go. No matter from what angle one viewed the situation, it was fraught with danger. The house itself – for all its beauty of décor and furnishing – seemed to be waiting like some strange presence holding its

20

breath. The family portraits on the walls looked down watchfully and with suspicion, as though privy to a secret which time alone would reveal. Carla did not deceive herself that she was immune from curiosity, or that the tingling sensation creeping over her body was entirely brought about by concern, or compassion, for the woman wanting her to risk the hazards of the mystery which built up like a mist rising from a bleak moor. It was like opening the pages of a book full of suspense and being powerless to put it down until the end had been reached. She said quietly, 'Very well. I'll stay. May I ask what Mr Ingram's attitude is about my coming here?'

'He is very pleased. I told him I thought I would advertise for someone.' She met Carla's gaze very steadily. 'I made quite sure that he did not see the advertisement. He was in the wilds of Scotland and the box number helped.' She added earnestly: 'It is difficult to explain, but he's quite detached from things not wholly concerned with himself. It isn't easy to know what he is thinking; but one is always aware of his disapproval. You will have to judge for yourself, of course.'

A momentary silence fell while Wells removed the tea tray. He seemed a rather formidable man, as though he, too, lived in shadow. His eyes were very dark and piercing, his eyebrows like the overhanging thatch of a roof and his face appeared to be indented from that point, his chin receding and losing itself in his neck without demarcation line. And while being waited on was a novelty and a luxury, Carla hoped that there might be times when she could enjoy making herself domestically useful. As the door shut on him, Vanessa Ingram said frankly, 'Wells and his wife resent your coming here, but I know you will overcome their prejudice. Having looked after me all my life, there's jealousy. They are wise enough to appreciate I am not their possession. On the other hand there are few, if any, people who would want to live here – beautiful though the setting is.'

'And do you want to live here?'

'I would live anywhere on earth if it could be without fear, or hurt. My husband likes it because it reflects something in him and whips up emotion… I'm telling you all this so badly and disjointedly, but it's impossible to put it into words. We have a few friends locally – particularly our solicitor, Adrian Grant.'

Carla could not resist the question, 'Couldn't you confide in him?'

'No, he and Melvin are friends. I prefer him to keep his illusions and he would never tolerate disloyalty.' She added swiftly, 'Which is what I am being now.' Her hands clenched in her lap. 'Perhaps you will understand as time goes on. All I know is that I shall feel much safer with you here.'

Carla understood. So often in life it was far easier to confide in a stranger than a friend. On the other hand she felt reasonably certain that she had been presented with a picture minus a frame. That intrigued her. Had she not instinctively liked Vanessa Ingram, she would not have given her promise to remain. *Instinctively.* The word leaped out at her. Who could apply logic or reason to such a reaction, any more than Vanessa Ingram could explain *why* she felt that her husband intended to murder her. She asked swiftly, 'Is Mr Ingram away at the moment?'

'Yes, but he returns this evening. Adrian Grant is coming to dinner.'

Again Carla recalled the advertisement, even if irrelevantly. 'Why did you specify secretarial qualifications?'

There was a second of uneasy silence before the reply came, 'Because I knew that would entail efficiency and an awareness of detail. Also, my husband has quite a number of letters to write. I type, but not up to any professional standard and often do more harm than good, because he gets so irritated. Do you mind fitting into that pattern on occasion?'

Carla smiled. 'On the contrary, I should

not like to lose the benefit of my training.'

'Then, there are the household accounts and things. I used to be very good at them, but fear has made me incompetent. I have no confidence left in myself – not in any direction.'

Carla felt an intense, overwhelming pity in that second. There was such starkness, such dejection, in the words and in the hopeless tone in which they were uttered that she said involuntarily, 'We shall have to alter that, Mrs Ingram.'

For the first time, a gleam of brightness flashed and then died away as a note of bitterness crept in; bitterness that lost itself in a spontaneous utterance, 'I feel you could almost work miracles ... but please call me Vanessa. Oh, yes. I hate the Mrs Ingram, it is so cold, so formal. You are doing me the favour by being here, certainly not I, you. If I cannot have a *friend* in this house, then I shall still have nothing. I think Carla is a lovely and unusual name. I had a sister and a brother,' she hurried on, following the trend of her own lonely thoughts. 'They were both killed instantly in one of those driving accidents which we read about as statistics, express regret, and take for granted.'

Perceptive, Carla knew that here was hurt to the point of agony. Never having known suffering, she tried to understand it and realised that only by living with it, could she hope to assess it. This was light and shade. She had to come to terms with both, appreciating that nothing in life was either black or white – merely a twilight of grey. She said quietly and with dignity, 'If this is how you feel, I am thankful to accept it. I detest surnames, anyway.'

At that moment there was a fluster and bustle in the hall, and in a matter of seconds Melvin Ingram walked through the door which Carla was watching, rather as a rabbit a stoat. Having greeted his wife, he stood before Carla and said warmly, 'Miss Selby.' Adding, 'I am so happy that you are here.'

Carla looked at him, trying to be purely objective. He was a tall handsome man, whose eyes were secretive and whose manner was charming. He looked at her with a frank friendliness which was a welcome in itself.

'I am happy to be here,' she exclaimed.

His gaze was penetrating. 'You certainly had a storm to battle through. I flew from Scotland to Exeter, having left the car there on the journey up. Saves so much time.'

Carla agreed. She was conscious of Vanessa sitting tense in a chair far too large for her. Her gaze did not leave her husband's face as she asked if he had enjoyed the trip and on being reminded that it was purely business, suggested the two were not always incompatible. At that he smiled indulgently and said: 'That is because you have never had anything to do with business, darling... Everything gone smoothly here?'

There was a rather disturbing and elusive quality in the way Melvin Ingram talked, for although he appeared to listen, Carla had the feeling that his thoughts were elsewhere and that after the initial commonplace utterances were over, he was restless and preoccupied. The word *murder* seemed to be flashing just above his head as she endeavoured to find in those first moments of appraisal some indication which either built up the fantastic idea, or destroyed it. There was a power about him and his voice was firm and decisive. She noticed that his hands were artistic, the fingers long. Had anyone ever been able to say that any hands were those of a potential murderer? She realised with faint shock that he was aware of her scrutiny and swiftly lowered her gaze.

'I'll bath and change,' he said, 'then we'll have a drink... No, dear, don't bother to come up; you stay with Miss Selby. Wells, if I know him, will have unpacked by now.'

A shadow passed over Vanessa's face. She wanted a few minutes alone with him, but managed to smile. 'Adrian is coming to dinner,' she said and paused before adding, 'I thought you would like that.'

'Oh, splendid.' He looked at Carla. 'I like foursomes as much as I dislike cocktail parties!' His laughter was spontaneous. Then, he added slowly, 'My wife has a very soft spot for Adrian – a very soft spot.' With that and an enigmatical smile, he went from the room.

No one could have said that there was anything offensive in his tone, but Carla saw Vanessa stiffen and there was pain in her eyes as she said, 'I *am* awfully fond of Adrian. He's a fine person.' She added meaningly, 'If ever Melvin talks like that I always feel it is to counteract some guilt complex in himself.'

'There is such a thing,' Carla warned, 'as judging people falsely and then mentally fitting everything they do, or say, to prove that judgement.'

Vanessa brightened. 'Perhaps being on one's own too much can stimulate the wrong thoughts. The lonely talk to themselves and probably never find the right answers to their own questions.'

Melvin returned to the room shortly afterwards, wearing a light, oatmeal palm beach type of suit and saying gaily, 'We undress for dinner in this house.' As he spoke, he took from his pocket a small packet wrapped in tissue paper and handed it to his wife, stooping and kissing her forehead as he said, 'I saw this in Perth, darling.'

Vanessa's face lit up and for a second she

knew the breath of happiness. 'Melvin, how lovely.' She opened it eagerly and finally drew out of an attractive white leather case a wrist watch. It was minute, delicate and gold. 'Oh, just what I wanted...' She put it on immediately. 'Such a surprise.' Her voice was full of warmth.

'Don't you usually have some gift whenever I go away?'

She hastened, 'Yes, but this is special – like a birthday.'

'That being the case then I think we'll have some champagne. I can hear Adrian's car. I always believe in finding things to celebrate.' He looked at Carla. His expression was significant. 'Finding you gives us an added reason.' He rang the bell, ordered the champagne and met Adrian as he was about to admit himself at the large front door. A privilege long accorded him.

Adrian Grant came into the room, bringing an atmosphere of security. He had a strong personality and a keen sense of humour, plus a ready wit. There was nothing in his manner to convey other than a relaxed friendship and he looked at Carla with instant approval, having dreaded the possibility of Vanessa engaging the wrong type.

In turn she studied him, liking the quiet thoughtfulness which lay behind more obvious characteristics. His eyes were his most striking feature, dark, almost magnetic. His mouth and jaw were firm, but his smile contradicted any suggestion of hardness. When he spoke his intonation had the attractiveness of a Scottish heritage, without trace of actual accent.

It was, thought Carla, an extraordinary situation and she found it difficult to believe that Adrian Grant would be either blind, or indifferent, to any grave defects in Melvin Ingram. She felt rather like a detective looking for hidden clues – in advance of the crime. They sat with the drinks which had been poured out by the host, talking easily. Vanessa proudly displayed her watch which Adrian admired and then, looking at Melvin, asked casually, 'A good trip?'

'Precious little of a trip about it. Keeping up with science these days is about as difficult as keeping track of a fly in the dark.'

'You can't be brilliant without some snags. Particularly as you get quite a bit of free travel thrown in.'

There was a rather heavy silence which Melvin broke by saying curtly, 'You seem particularly interested in that phase.'

Carla saw Vanessa tense and fear flash into her eyes.

'Just envy,' Adrian explained with a smile. 'Country solicitors seem to find most of their clients on their doorstep.'

The atmosphere changed. Melvin's laughter rang out. He looked pleased. 'Never really could understand why you've remained in St Austell.'

'Probably for much the same reason that you like living at Polvose. You must like Cornwall even more than I to have made it your permanent home.' Adrian looked at Carla, as he said, 'Now we have someone else to convert.'

'I think I'm a convert already. Driving up here in that storm could hardly leave one indifferent.'

'A royal welcome,' Melvin suggested. He shot Carla the question disconcertingly. 'Have you been accustomed to near isolation?'

Was that suspicion, Carla asked herself, or merely her own awareness of every word uttered because of what Vanessa had told her? She explained about Ascot and her previous job. Melvin held his head slightly to one side, listening intently and she felt that there was a note of interrogation about his final, 'So, coming here was in the nature of a whim?'

Carla glanced at Vanessa who was mutely pleading with her not to bring in the word, adventure. She smiled. 'Just that and boredom with tycoons. I can always return.'

Melvin sensed the note of determination, even of pride, in her voice. 'Heaven forbid. I like people who decide to do things that are unusual and new to them. Nothing like a

30

spirit of adventure,' he finished smoothly.

Carla commented, 'If you could call coming here that.' Did he know the wording of Vanessa's advertisement, despite her belief that he had not seen it?

Adrian, suddenly watchful, said, 'We must prove to you that we can turn almost anything on in Cornwall. Pixies, adventure! Just name it. Who knows you might marry and settle down here – or does that sound too dull?'

'I'll answer that question if the situation should arise,' she retorted blithely.

Melvin refilled their glasses and, having handed Carla hers, said, 'What were your first impressions of Polvose – apart from the storm?' His gaze was searching.

'Mysterious,' she replied without hesitation. 'I imagine its history would be interesting.'

'You imagine right,' Adrian put in.

'All the better.' Carla smiled at Vanessa flashing her reassurance. 'I love old houses and conjuring up visions of former owners.'

'The romantic type,' Melvin spoke without ridicule. 'I cannot imagine your being afraid of anything. Good in an emergency, too.'

Carla broke the sudden silence with a bantering laugh,

'You forget, Mr Ingram, that I have been a confidential secretary. You certainly have to be good in emergencies and not afraid of anything – or anyone!'

'The soul of discretion,' chuckled Adrian.

Vanessa saw Melvin frown, knowing that look of darkness in his eyes and in order to divert the conversation said, 'By the way, Ella Fairbright had a son this morning.'

Carla was watching and saw Melvin's temper rise for a fraction of a second before he managed to comment, 'Darling, has that anything to do with secretaries?'

'Yes,' Vanessa flashed back, 'Ella was his before they married!'

At that Melvin roared with laughter. 'Good for you! And good for them. They wanted a boy.' He continued to laugh and then added, 'You've already sent flowers, if I know you.'

Vanessa explained to Carla that the Fairbrights were friends of theirs who lived in Fowey and had been married five years, wanting children badly.

'Something,' Melvin exclaimed, 'I can never enthuse about – children.'

'Few men can,' Adrian said easily, 'until they have their own.'

Vanessa was completely natural, although Carla knew she was fighting to be so. 'I shall have to put Melvin to the test, shan't I?'

Melvin's voice was gentle as he exclaimed, 'Anytime, if that makes you happy.'

Carla stared at Adrian. Was it possible that

he, as a solicitor, failed to appreciate the curious atmosphere and tensions? Was that impassive attitude a form of retreat because he knew too much – or too little? *'My wife has a very soft spot for Adrian – a very soft spot.'* The words echoed through the tunnel of her mind like the booming sound of a megaphone. Already she knew she was committed to an experience which only time would clarify. There was something about Melvin that was undeniably attractive. An elusiveness perhaps allied to an alert sinister mind. The question was, why should he wish to murder his wife? And how was she going to decide how near to truth, or hallucination, Vanessa had come?

It was after dinner that Adrian suggested showing Carla 'the estate' as he jokingly called it.

The light was fading from the sky and, in the approaching darkness, there was all the mystery of the unknown. Woods, copses, the creek far below – all seemed touched with magic. The trees, with their tracery of bright green leaves, were like a courtesan hiding her face behind a feathery fan. Faint mists rose from the grounds spreading like pale ghosts. In that strange twilight, all the blossom seemed to quiver like dancing children – young, gay and full of promise. Only the house stood in shadow, its lighted windows peering, rather than looking, out on the panorama.

Carla said deliberately, indicating a certain spot on the granite walls, 'That must be my bedroom.' She watched Adrian's expression carefully, aware of his obvious surprise which amounted almost to consternation. 'Oh, I know someone fell from that window and was killed.' Her voice sounded matter of fact.

Adrian said a trifle grimly, 'No doubt Mrs Wells supplied that information.'

Carla looked innocent. 'Most thought-fully.'

'She and her husband are remarkable retainers.' There was a rather astringent note in his voice. Quite apart from anything else, he wondered just why the girl beside him should have been given that particular room – next to Melvin's and Vanessa's – when there was another, with bathroom, on the other side of the house.

Carla avoided making an issue of the matter. She laughed, as she said, 'I neither fall, nor am I pushed, out of windows!' Her gaze met his. 'The story, were it not tragic, lends colour to this whole place. There must be some incredible legends about it.'

He looked at her with a rather unnerving directness. 'May I be impertinent and ask just why you really came down here?'

The question staggered her because it seemed full of innuendo. She retorted stiffly, 'I'm very sorry, Mr Grant, but my coming here was precisely as I explained before dinner. Or is your memory at fault? For a solicitor—'

'I'm sorry,' he hastened, 'no man and certainly no solicitor, should ask the wrong questions.'

Carla's anger died down and she replied quietly, 'It was not the question, but its implication that annoyed me.'

His smile was irresistible. 'I'm sorry; forgive me.'

'Have I any alternative?' Her laughter was low and provocative.

'None!' For all that, Adrian wanted to be understood, yet not to betray. His gaze held hers inescapably. 'I think you can appreciate that one's profession, or job, dominates one's outlook. A solicitor expects lies and is, alas, always looking for flaws. Just as a secretary protects her employer and anticipates his needs – including keeping time-wasters away from him.'

Carla gave a nod of approval. 'Actually, my being here is a spur of the moment decision. I was tired of keeping time-wasters away and living and breathing only money – much as I love all the good things it can buy. I hope I shall be successful here.'

Adrian looked at her intently. 'If you can give Mrs Ingram friendship and companionship, you will remove much of her loneliness. Melvin has an exacting job, with great responsibility. He has to be away a good deal. She has been amazingly helpful and good about it all, but I've felt recently that she was nearing breaking point. She needs to get out more. This is a glorious place, but beauty can sometimes make one feel even lonelier. I cannot quite understand why Melvin was so set on coming to Polvose, but that is none of my business. For my own part, I could not be more pleased they are here... I must say that you are a very pleasant surprise! I had pictured, or visualised, someone drably efficient. Don't ask me why.'

Carla wondered what would happen if she were to tell him the truth of the situation as Vanessa had outlined it.

At that moment, Melvin rushed out of the house. 'Miss Selby, will you please come to my wife. She is not feeling well. Oh, nothing to be alarmed about. She has these semi-fainting fits from time to time.' He glanced at Adrian, adding, 'As you know.'

Adrian was about to suggest that he did not know, but thought better of it.

Carla hurried into the house. Vanessa was lying on the sofa, white, drawn, trembling.

'I'm all right.' The words came on a breath of pain. 'I begged Melvin not to fetch you in.'

Carla was not deceived. She could see the

throbbing of the vein in Vanessa's neck and knew that, could she have taken her pulse, it would have been racing. 'Have you a doctor near?'

Vanessa sat up, her eyes wild and terrorised. 'Never mention doctors. Melvin will not have one in the house.'

Carla's anger rose. 'But that's absurd. Would he allow people to die to protect his own prejudice?' She put a hand up to her mouth, aware of the significant meaning of the words, *to die.*

Vanessa stretched out a hand. 'Don't be upset. But the answer to your question, is not "allow" but *desire.* I suppose when he gets into one of his rages, I'm so scared, so frightened, that I go to pieces.' She got up restlessly as she spoke. 'If you knew what a relief it is to have you here. Even now I feel better. Before, I was so completely shut away with my own heartache and morbid thoughts. Oh, that's true; the quotation that "conscience doth make cowards of us all" might well have a substitute word – loneliness.' She drew in her breath as though it were an effort, before adding, 'Mental loneliness.'

Carla would like to have brought in the suggestion that emotional loneliness could come into the same category. But she did not speak, because she sensed that a confidence was to follow as Vanessa went close

37

to the long windows, pulled aside the heavy old-gold curtains and peered out, making certain that Melvin was not about to return in a matter of seconds. Then, she looked at Carla. 'You've a right to know the facts,' she said, honestly. 'It was about your sleeping in the room adjoining ours.'

Carla looked bewildered and then exclaimed involuntarily, 'Because of the window?' Even as she spoke she felt a shudder of fear.

Vanessa said frankly, 'No; his excuse was that he disliked your being next door to us. I know differently,' she added in a low, frightened voice. 'That is why I gave the room to you. I feel protected and I'm certain you will be careful.'

Carla asked, 'Are you accustomed to going into that room?'

Vanessa's answer was, in itself, an explanation. 'Oh, yes. I love to look down on the creek and see the tops of the trees at window level. It is so beautiful – like music. Melvin used to feel the same.'

'Used to?'

'Yes.' She made a gesture of despair. 'No one can really explain all this and I should not blame you if you packed and left the house tonight. But I had a strange feeling just now that he sensed I knew what was in his mind. Even brilliant men realise that a woman can know by *instinct* what they

38

cannot discover by reason. Perhaps in this, they are always at a disadvantage.'

Carla suggested firmly, 'For all that, a woman's imagination can run away with her. Every human being has some queer pattern of behaviour. That watch on your arm – it gave you great pleasure. And when even the question of children arose, your husband–'

'We've been married for seven years, Carla. Melvin *says* these things, but he would have hated children. I love him more than having children. I suppose I ought quietly to resign myself to this situation. But when he raves at me and says the most appalling things that are so unjust … I go to pieces. I told you I was weak.' She added, 'You have never been in love – really in love – have you?'

'No – just happy flirtations.'

Vanessa – hearing Melvin and Adrian at the front door – said in a whisper, 'Then try never to fall in love with the wrong person. That is the greatest hell on earth.'

Melvin and Adrian returned at that moment. Carla was aware of a faint irritation in Melvin's voice as he asked how Vanessa was feeling. An irritation which vanished and turned to a gentle concern within a matter of minutes. Carla reflected that, should Melvin intend to murder his wife, the alibi of fainting fits would make a fall from the window likely – but not suspicious. His annoyance at having the room occupied could well be an intrusion on his plans. It struck her, also, as being rather odd that, after one tragedy, there should not be bars at that particular window to prevent any further accidents.

Melvin said firmly, 'I think you should see a doctor, Vanessa. I know how averse you are to doing so, but–'

Vanessa gasped, '*I* am averse! You are the one who dislikes even the idea of having a doctor in the house at all!'

Melvin studied her with an indulgence that might have been given to a child. 'Well, of course, darling, if you like to believe that, there is nothing more to be said – is there? Adrian, what about a night cap?'

Adrian refused. Carla noticed the glances he shot rather anxiously in Vanessa's direction. Was there some secret bond between these two and was Melvin jealous? Question after question chased through her mind, not the least being why should Melvin suggest Vanessa consulting a doctor if what she had said were true about his general attitude? She, Carla, felt that she was listening to a defence in advance the whole time.

As Adrian left, he said to her, 'When you have some spare time, may I show you some of our beauty spots?' He held her gaze and she felt a little tingle of excitement to which was allied relief that she might, in emergency, have someone outside the house to help her.

This man, as the family solicitor, would certainly be privy to some of the secrets and the skeletons. She said naturally, 'I'd love that.'

The sound of his car driving away, its last echo gone, left a well of silence in the room. Melvin stood, glass in hand, looking out of the one window over which the curtains had not been drawn. There was a faraway expression in his eyes. Then, he said abruptly, almost curtly, 'You must be tired, Vanessa.'

'You far more than I,' she replied gently, although the tone of his voice withered her. 'I suppose it is getting late.' She glanced at Carla as she spoke, avoiding the steely glint in Melvin's eyes.

Carla got to her feet. She was emotionally exhausted, rather than tired. It seemed that she had been at Polvose a month instead of a matter of hours. 'A long drive and Cornish air,' she commented, 'certainly make one delightfully sleepy.'

'We have breakfast about eight-thirty,' Vanessa said. 'Oh, and morning tea about quarter to eleven.'

Carla wished them both good night. As she reached the hall, Mrs Wells detached herself from the shadows of a corridor leading to the kitchen. She stood, solid and inscrutable, her voice without trace of expression as she acknowledged Carla's pleasant, 'Good night, Mrs Wells.' Carla had the feeling that this woman probably managed to sleep with one eye open so that nothing escaped her.

The house seemed almost frighteningly still as Carla shut her bedroom door. She thought of her parents and Ascot, deciding that she would write them a long letter before the morning tea arrived. It was obvious that she could not divulge the fantastic story of Polvose, because she had not made up her own mind about it. When finally she slid between the cool sheets, she stretched like a slinky, purring cat.

She was awakened by the sound of a man's voice thundering through the silence and, glancing at her travelling clock, realised that she had not been asleep for more than ten minutes. It was obviously Melvin and came from downstairs. Swiftly, she got out of bed and went to one of the wide open windows, just in time to see Vanessa running down the long drive, her slim figure pricked out in the moonlight, and what struck Carla most was the fact that she had her hands cupped over her ears, as though she could not bear to hear any more. Melvin emerged and stood watching, the glow of his cigarette obvious.

Carla felt that her heart had stopped beating and she pressed back against the curtains so that, should he look up, she would not be visible. For a second or two he waited and then called out sharply, 'Vanessa!' And again, 'Vanessa.'

Would that retreating form stop? And if not, where was its destination? Why did Melvin stand there like a statue and was *his* idea of murder to drive his wife to suicide? Carla kept her gaze upon that vanishing figure; a figure which the moonlight illuminated eerily. Even the countryside seemed pregnant with mystery and fear. Then, suddenly – almost as though by remote control – Vanessa stopped. She remained with her back to the house for a few dramatic seconds and then turned, as though mesmerised and walked, trance-like, back to where Melvin awaited her. He completely ignored her and went into the house. Vanessa followed. A door shut and all was still.

Carla crept noiselessly back to bed.

2

Breakfast, the following morning, was particularly harmonious – much to Carla's surprise. Melvin appeared to be in the best of spirits and Vanessa had lost the air of sadness which had characterised her the previous day. No mention was made of the incident that Carla had witnessed. She told herself that these two people might well be the type who fought, indulged in flights of

43

fantasy, but enjoyed a passionate reconciliation. Despite herself, she found Melvin both amusing and charming. The sardonic humour, the barbed references, had given place to a good-tempered banter, tinged with discreet flattery, towards Vanessa. Finally, he asked her, 'Now where would you like me to take you today? It's perfect weather for bathing, picnicking – anything. We can even hop across to the north coast and surf, if you like.'

Carla saw the light of fear that flashed momentarily into Vanessa's eyes. 'Not surfing,' she hastened.

He did not argue, just inclined his head in acceptance. Then he looked at Carla. 'What would you like to do?'

Carla laughed spontaneously, 'I thought I was here to work.'

'Not while I'm at home for the next few days,' he said firmly. 'Do you surf?'

'Nothing so thrilling, alas. I swim, ride and dance. Oh, I can cook and am domesticated. There my meagre qualifications end.' She found Melvin's gaze disconcerting and added swiftly, 'Apart, of course, from my work.'

'This is a far cry from Ascot and London,' he suggested, his gaze still upon her.

'Which makes it the more interesting. Monotony kills even incentive.'

Melvin suddenly switched back to the

question of bathing, suggesting that Carla might enjoy a lesson in surfing and that, once Vanessa was in the water, she would enjoy it as she used to do.

Vanessa tried to conceal her sudden nervousness and, as in all moments of stress, said the wrong thing. 'It would be fun if Adrian could join us. Make a foursome.'

Carla felt the temperature drop several degrees. Melvin got up from the table and said stiffly, 'By all means. I'm sure you will find the courage to surf with *him.*' With that he crossed to the telephone which stood on a small table, got through to Adrian, and emphasised how anxious Vanessa was for him to join them adding that, since it was Saturday, the question of work did not arise.

At the other end of the line, Adrian was smiling his appreciation and accepted with alacrity. As he put the receiver down, he glanced at Clark Faber (his friend and business partner with whom he shared a house which perched itself up on the cliffs at Porthpean – a house which he, himself, owned), and said, 'You know, Clark, there's something strange going on at Polvose. This girl, Carla Selby, whom I told you about last night … I can't get the hang of why she should come down here like this.'

Clark Faber was one of those easygoing men who, at forty, felt that nothing was ever half as important, or as serious, as it appeared. His tolerance was not indifference, it was a built in belief that no one could accurately assess the motives, or emotions, of another human being. He smiled slowly and reached for his pipe. He looked as comfortable as a spaniel lying on a rug in front of a roaring fire on a winter's day. 'Why try to get the hang of it? She has her reasons, no doubt. And all your guesses won't prove anything. As for there being something strange going on at Polvose, there is always something strange going on in every house in the land!' He pushed the last threads of tobacco down, struck his match and looked at Adrian even as he puffed out an amazing amount of smoke, 'I'll give you this, I've always had the feeling that it was a sinister house, filled with violence.' For just that second Clark was jerked out of his easy acceptance of life – almost as though his statement came involuntarily.

Adrian looked shocked and staggered. 'Good God, coming from *you*–'

'Um-m,' Clark's head nodded as he appeared to focus on some object at a far corner of the room. 'Must be something I ate for breakfast.'

Adrian made a deprecating sound. 'Nonsense. Damn it, we're both friends of the Ingrams.'

'So we are. What does that prove?' He took his pipe from his mouth and smoothed the bowl of it before adding, 'But what do we know *about* them? Ever thought of that? You see now why I always think it so much more comfortable not to try to fathom the depths of a character. There's always a closed door at the bottom.'

A sinister house, filled with violence.

Adrian stared at Clark disbelievingly. Every word he had uttered was foreign to his conception of the man he had known for most of his life.

Clark chuckled. 'See what I mean? Your ideas about me are the direct result of my attitude towards life. You know I'm not a liar, a thief, or a crook and that I don't get ruffled. You know the colour of my politics and that I like tennis and golf and have never had any great desire to get married, or have any offspring. All those things may tell you everything – but do they?'

'No,' Adrian agreed, somewhat abashed. He had prided himself that he knew Clark backwards.

Clark got up from his chair. 'The trouble with solicitors is that we think we know people; we don't! We know their crimes, moral lapses and their *attitude*. But their ill-assorted mixture of feelings, emotions, even ideas... Not a damn thing. Now I'll go and see if I can beat old Jimmy Bartok. And what do I know about *him* after fifteen years? That he plays better golf than I, stands his rounds, is apparently happily married and has three children. That's enough for comfort! I don't mean the children, but from the point of view of our relationship!' He reached the door and looked back over his shoulder. 'Don't forget what I said about Polvose. And watch your step. I'm eating at the club tonight.' With that, he swung out of the room.

Adrian lit a cigarette and muttered to himself, 'Well, I'll be damned!'

Back at Polvose, Vanessa was saying to Carla (Melvin having gone out to speak to Woods, the gardener), 'Please don't give Melvin the impression that you would like to surf.' A rather wild look came into Vanessa's eyes as she added, 'The last time Melvin took me out surfing, I was nearly drowned.' The words echoed significantly through the silence.

Carla asked urgently, 'Are you *sure* – really sure – about all this?'

'Quite sure.' Her voice was quiet and the more dramatic for that reason. 'Shall I say that I don't want it to be a case of third time lucky – for *him.*'

Carla felt an upsurge of anger and indignation that manifested itself finally in her cry, 'But why *stay?*'

'Because of the lesser of evils. Dying would be preferable to living without him. And there are times when everything seems perfect and the rest just a bad dream.'

Carla wondered why no reference had been made to the episode of last night. What had Melvin been raving about? She thought it better not to broach the subject lest it cause Vanessa distress. Adrian's arrival came as a relief and Vanessa whispered, 'I'm going to leave you alone with him. Tell him not to enthuse about bathing. He'll know what I mean.'

Carla said, 'Then he *does* understand your fears.'

'No, no! Not in that sense – only how persistent Melvin can be when he gets an idea into his head. And how carefully he has to be handled if he doesn't get his own way.' With that, she hurried through a door leading from the dining-room into Melvin's study.

Carla noticed the way Adrian glanced around, having greeted her, and said, 'Vanessa?' He might have been looking for his wife, as is the custom of most men the moment they enter the house.

Carla gave a hasty explanation and then said deliberately, suspicion creeping upon her, 'I can fetch Vanessa if you wish.'

He looked slightly uncomfortable. 'Nothing urgent.'

Carla mentioned the bathing as discreetly as she could. It brought a defensive reaction from Adrian. 'If Melvin likes to be spartan –

49

fine. It's far too early for bathing. Or do you disagree?'

'Not entirely. In England it is a question of weather, not of which month it happens to be, but I shall fall in with Vanessa's wishes.'

The day was not a success. Melvin tried to conceal his displeasure because no one wanted to accompany him into the water and, after an acrimonious discussion, they ended up by lunching at the Fowey Hotel, which Carla felt must be one of the most beautiful spots in Cornwall. They sat having their cocktails, looking out not only to sea, but across the river to hills that rose from the water's edge and where sheep and cattle grazed. The sky was an Indian blue and the general atmosphere made it difficult to believe that one was actually in England. It was spoiled for Carla by the undercurrent between Melvin and Vanessa. He spoke sharply and often scathingly and when Adrian attempted to introduce a more pleasant note, it was to be met with argument and dissension. Vanessa became more and more quiet and finally ceased to talk at all. After the atmosphere that had prevailed at breakfast that morning, Carla felt an increasing unreality. Her position was not made more comfortable by the fact that Melvin could not have been more charming to her, personally. Several times she intercepted the significant glances exchanged by

50

Adrian and Vanessa. It did not escape her notice that Melvin was also mindful of them.

When they returned to Polvose, Carla expected Adrian to leave and he was half way through an excuse to do so when Vanessa begged him to stay for dinner. In her welcoming voice, there was a note of defiance. To Carla's surprise, Melvin was insistent, suggesting that the evening might make up for the anti-climax of the outing generally. Again the mood changed and laughter returned. It was in the middle of dinner that Melvin said, casually, 'I shall probably have to fly over to Paris for a couple of days. Maybe next week.' He looked at Vanessa. 'At least now I can leave you in good hands.'

The telephone rang at that moment and immediately Melvin got to his feet. 'That will be Sir Charles. I'll take it in the study,' he said. 'Probably to cancel the trip, now I've mentioned it!'

But it wasn't anything of the kind and Carla felt, as she listened to his rather lengthy explanation of the call, that there was something about it which did not ring true. There was also a grimness about him, as though at some entirely different level he had been thwarted for the second time that day.

'No one can say that Melvin's life is lacking in variety,' Adrian commented a little later when he and Carla were alone in the

51

sitting-room.

'I'm sure it all works very well.'

'I seem to be out of favour today,' he murmured without malice.

They looked at each other and a sudden spark of emotion silenced them. It was as though an overwhelming and swift desire wiped out time and place, making the fact that they had met only yesterday unimportant. Adrian said urgently, 'Carla, there is one thing you must know–'

His words froze as a spine-chilling cry went through the house like thunder. Vanessa's voice was shrill and terrified, as she called for help.

Adrian and Carla moved like people jet propelled. All that registered in Carla's mind was the window in her bedroom and she raced up the stairs, Adrian following. Vanessa was on the floor, her hands clawing the windowsill. She was half fainting, incoherent, but in that incoherency, her terrified voice cried, 'Someone … tried… I–'

At that point, she fainted.

Carla looked around as Adrian lifted Vanessa from the floor and put her on the bed. Melvin seemed to be missing and then the sound of his and Mrs Wells' voices broke the sudden uncanny silence. A second later he rushed into the room and to Vanessa's side. 'I was walking along the cliff path,' he said breathlessly, 'when I heard Vanessa cry out. What happened?'

Vanessa stirred, opened her eyes and, seeing Melvin, whimpered, 'There was someone in the house; someone tried to push me out of the window.'

Mrs Wells appeared like a dark shadow haunting the open doorway. She heard Vanessa's remark and murmured, her expression malevolent, 'We'll search–'

Melvin said with authority, 'You might as well look for a needle in the maze at Hampton Court... But thank you, all the same.' He looked down at Vanessa and while his voice was gentle, his eyes were cold. 'What were you doing in Carla's room, anyway? And why is that window wide open?'

Carla felt icy fingers on her spine. She had left the window almost closed.

Adrian said sympathetically, 'Wouldn't it be better if Vanessa told us about it a little later? The shock–'

Melvin retorted, 'My questions are simple enough.'

Vanessa looked at him with a strange remoteness. 'I came to put those roses in the room.' She indicated a vase on the dressing table.

Carla could not stay the observation, 'There was no light on when we found you.'

For a second it was as though all the air had been sucked from the room. The atmosphere was heavy with suspicion.

'Someone turned it off,' Vanessa whispered in a low, dread voice. 'I was by the window. All I saw was a shadow – not even that really. For a second, I thought the lights had fused.' She covered her face with her hands. 'It was horrible.'

Melvin might have been a wood carving, rather than a man, as he persisted, 'Did you open that window?'

Carla held her breath.

Vanessa said simply: 'Yes, I opened it. I love to look down on the creek when it's all dark and quiet. The rocks have a special life of their own. Looking through glass isn't the same – not to me.'

Melvin scoffed: 'You and your fanciful ideas! Well! This may teach you a lesson.'

'Such as?' Adrian asked a trifle curtly.

Melvin got up from the side of the bed. 'Such as not to allow imagination to get the better of you,' he answered with an air of finality.

Vanessa protested, 'And did imagination turn off the light?'

His lips twitched into a rather pitying smile. 'No, it allowed you to believe you turned it on in the first place.'

Adrian exclaimed, 'Really, Melvin!'

Melvin changed his attitude slightly. 'Someone has to protect Vanessa from herself. She wanders through this place at dusk as though she has the eyes of a cat. I've warned her many times about it.' He looked at Carla and there was admiration in his gaze. 'It might be a good idea if you kept the door of this room locked!' His tone was half bantering and yet Carla felt that a note of seriousness lay beneath it.

Adrian indicated a second door at the far side of the room. 'Where does that lead to?'

Melvin hastened, 'It's blind. I believe it once led to the roof. We've never used it.'

Carla said, 'I'd be curious to know its secrets.'

Vanessa had moved from the bed and stood beside Melvin. She was still white and Carla noticed that her hands were clenched. It was obvious that she was making a supreme effort to regain control. Her gaze sought Melvin's with a hunger that was poignant. Her voice was unsteady as she said, 'I'm sorry to have been so silly. Forgive me.'

Melvin put his arm about her shoulders. 'I think what you need is a drink,' he said amiably.

Carla recalled Adrian's last words to her before Vanessa's cry smashed into their conversation, *'Carla, there is one thing you must know–'* She glanced at him over her shoulder as they filed out of the bedroom, hoping for some sign which might betray a little of what he was feeling and finding only an inscrutability. One thing stood out in her mind about the episode she had just witnessed –

the adroit manner in which Melvin had taken the fight into Vanessa's camp, avoiding any cross questioning. Yet he had volunteered the information that he had been walking along the cliff path when Vanessa shrieked. Again, suspicion stabbed; at no time had he suggested informing the police, even if only as a precautionary measure. She found the courage to say when they returned to the sitting-room, 'My first reaction to all that has happened, was to telephone the police.' She added firmly, 'Better inform them of twenty unnecessary scares, than let one criminal through the net.'

Melvin flicked the ash from his cigarette in a little nervous gesture. 'I agree with you.'

Vanessa hurriedly changed the conversation. Her gaze darted apprehensively towards Melvin, seeking some gentleness in his expression – without avail. He lapsed into a stony silence and the evening dragged to an end. Adrian was thankful when he reached his car and was about to set off on the homeward journey. Carla ran out suddenly and stood beside the open window at the driving seat. 'Adrian,' she asked breathlessly, 'you said there was something I should know... What?'

He hedged and she realised it. His smile did not deceive her. 'It could be that I fell in love with you at first sight,' he answered quietly.

'Only it isn't.'

His gaze drew hers to his in a long, disconcerting look. 'You could be wrong about that,' he said almost roughly. 'Have a meal with me tomorrow evening, Carla. We can talk then.'

'Not tomorrow,' she replied swiftly, 'I'd like to keep an eye on Vanessa. Monday?'

'Very well.' He put the clutch in.

Melvin appeared at the front door. 'Lingering farewells,' he said with an empty laugh.

'No law against them,' Adrian retorted and drove slowly away, calling out to Carla, 'Monday at seven. I'll collect you.'

Melvin lit a cigarette and remained standing outside the house. 'A word of advice, Carla,' he began quietly, 'don't take the dramatics tonight too seriously. If I'd thought for one second that Vanessa had been attacked, I should have sent for the police. As it is, she is a very highly strung, emotional type and, for some reason best known to herself, that window has always held a morbid fascination for her. I'm sorry your introduction to Polvose has been so stormy. I must admit that I'm scared you may not care to stay.' He looked down at her very intently. 'I shall have to rely on Adrian's charm to plead my cause.'

'I don't think that will be necessary and I'll let you know well in advance if I should want to go.' She added deliberately, 'I find it very difficult to believe that Vanessa's morbid fascination caused her to faint as she did.' Carla dare not press the matter too far, but she wanted to make him aware that she possessed certain powers of observation and deduction. On the face of it, there would appear to be very little chance of his being guilty, for there was no question that he had come into the house, spoken to Mrs Wells, after the incident. What she wanted to discover was whether he could have left the bedroom by some method known only to himself, escaped detection and then returned as though his stroll along the cliff walk had been interrupted by Vanessa's cry. She decided that she must explore that walk and time herself over the distance. Meanwhile, she watched Melvin closely, her eyes attuned to the blue velvet darkness. He was alert and suspicious.

'Have you any special theory of your own?' he asked tersely.

'None that I could prove.'

He began to speak and then stopped. As they were about to re-enter the house, he said firmly, 'I'd like to emphasise every word I've uttered – no matter what you may theorise.'

Carla made no comment, but she was aware of Melvin's irritation which, in itself, she regarded as defensive. Yet, as he walked away from her and went into his study, a curious pang of regret touched her. In different circumstances he could have been a friend. That automatically brought her thoughts to Adrian and his remark about love at first sight. Emotion sharpened at the possibility and then died on the breath of anxiety. If he were in love with Vanessa what more subtle technique could he employ than to create a diversion by way of herself? She found anger welling unexpectedly and she hurried into the sitting-room conscious of having neglected her duties. Vanessa was asleep on the sofa. She looked so pale, so wan, that for an agonising second, Carla thought of death.

'Carla...' the voice was drowsy and muffled. 'You know what happened and ... who it ... was.'

Carla's mouth felt dry and her heart quickened its beat. There was something uncanny about the utterance, the more so since it became a secret shared – another secret. Vanessa jerked herself into a sitting position, stared about her almost as though unaware of her surroundings. Seeing Carla brought an expression of relief. She whispered, 'Where is *he?*'

'In the study.'

'I'll go up to bed. I feel safer there.' She got up unsteadily and forced a smile. 'If I pretend to be asleep, nothing more will be said about any of this.'

Carla protested, 'No woman can stand such a situation.'

'A woman in love always believes in miracles,' Vanessa murmured wistfully.

Carla did not deceive herself about Melvin's powers of attraction. She felt the passion and the misery of the woman by her side. A few minutes later she saw her up the stairs and then waited, still dressed, in her own room until the house had taken to itself that deep silence which comes mysteriously once its occupants sleep. Then, hardly daring to breathe, she crept down into the hall and made her way to a side door which was away from the upstairs rooms. The lock turned, the bolt went back and suddenly she found herself in the grounds. The grass killed all sound and she trod warily, keeping on it until she had left the house behind. A house which was a dark shadow against the night sky. *The cliff walk,* she kept repeating to herself, almost as though by doing so she would discover its direction. Suddenly, almost perilously, a narrow pathway came into view. It was steep and forbidding, its surface rough and stony. The cliff face rose sheer to her right and the waters of the creek loomed below. There was no protection from that deadly drop. Yet its danger held fascination. She realised that she was now in line with her own bedroom and nearer the house than when she started. The question was could anyone looking out of her bedroom window see her as she stood there? Looking up gave a clearer view than looking down on a tortuous path.

A sound nearby made every nerve in her body tingle; a shiver rather like an electric shock went down her spine. The darkness was no longer impenetrable, because her eyes had become attuned to it. Footsteps … footsteps coming nearer. Who would be likely to be out at this hour, or at this spot? She stood still and trembling, pressing against the cliffs, afraid of what she might see, as though even a human shape might take to itself the sinister happenings of the night. The bend ahead hid the approaching figure and she was too paralysed with fright to attempt to run. And then suddenly she saw Adrian…

3

Carla saw Adrian hurry towards her and a rather sick sensation of distrust cut across her relief because it was he and not some formidable attacker. What was he doing there? Precisely the same question shot through his mind and he found that jealousy spiked him. For a second they stared at each other in grim accusation. Then he demanded, 'For heaven's sake why come wandering here at this hour?'

'I could reverse the question,' she retorted.

'My answer would be simple. I wanted to spy out the land here and make quite certain that no one was prowling around.'

'Do you imagine they would come along this walk for your benefit?'

He urged her a few paces forward and pointed to a deep cavern in the cliff. 'You could hide anything – or anyone – there.'

Carla shivered. 'Ugh, it makes me feel creepy.' She clung to him as he was about to enter it. The sudden contact of his body against hers awakened an emotion dangerously new. She drew back apologetically, but before she could speak he leaned down, his lips meeting hers in a swift, but passionate, kiss. 'No apologies needed – I hope on either side.' His voice was low and seemed to linger on the wind which was fresh from the sea. The beauty of the scene became a transmutation of the momentary harmony between them. 'Not on either side,' she murmured, a little shaken by her own vulnerability.

His attitude changed as he asked, almost gravely, 'What *did* bring you here, Carla?'

'Curiosity,' she answered because it was as near the truth as she dared get. 'I like exploring places.'

'Without an objective?' His expression suggested disbelief. 'Or were you looking for prowlers? Rather a dangerous pastime in a place like this.'

'I was certainly not looking for prowlers,' she said emphatically. 'Perhaps the events of the evening had made me restless. It was hardly a pleasant experience and *someone* must have been responsible for Vanessa's terror. Is this area all owned by Melvin?'

'Yes.' He changed his attitude. 'Back to the house for you. You're cold.'

'What are you going to do?'

'See you safely in.' He sounded bantering. His hand brushed her arm as they walked together. And as he noiselessly opened the side door so that she could creep back into the house, it suddenly seemed a long while until Monday. He whispered, 'I'll ring you on Monday. We shall both know the best time, then.'

The door closed and as she locked and bolted it, she felt that her heart was thumping so loudly that it must shatter the deep silence that filled the darkness. One fact registered even above the emotional turmoil: Melvin could not have got back from the cliff walk in the space of time between Vanessa's cry and his entry into the room. She had not needed a watch to time the distance. The sound of a board creaking set her nerves tingling. Not wanting to be discovered wandering about the house, she refrained from turning on a light and put out her pencil torch, standing quite still. But all was quiet and she flashed the torch on again, trying to find the courage to make her way through the wilderness of space to her own room. The staircase, when she reached it, seemed twice as long as she remembered it. Every door on the landing appeared to be a watchful eye. The safety of her own room became luxury.

It was on Monday morning that Melvin, having read his mail, announced that he had to leave for Paris that day. He would fly to London from Exeter and leave by a night plane. A seat had already been booked for him, but he would get details once he contacted Sir Charles. He looked at Vanessa and smiled. 'I'll be in Paris for a couple of days and telephone you when I get back to London. We've a conference on Thursday and that will enable me to get home for the weekend. Worked in rather well. You can show Carla some of our beauty spots.' He looked extremely happy as he added, 'What a relief it is not to be leaving you here alone, darling.'

Vanessa smiled. She felt bleak and empty. So many questions darted through her mind to which she dare not give utterance.

'I'll bring you a large bottle of Magi.' Melvin spoke indulgently, but he already had the air of a man far away.

'Lovely,' Vanessa exclaimed. 'I'll go and see about your packing.'

He got up from the breakfast table. 'No need, darling. I'll tell Wells to look after it.' He paused a second. 'Must get away as quickly as possible.'

Carla asked casually, 'Are the flight services frequent from Exeter?'

Melvin hurried over the words, 'Up to a point, yes. I never know these things. That's the best of having a secretary. Mine's a wizard. She has an electronic brain!' He added the last remark as he went from the room.

Vanessa slid a registered parcel into Carla's hand. 'Put that in my desk, will you? It's something on approval for Melvin's birthday. I don't want him to know about it... I think I'll make certain that Wells doesn't forget anything for the trip.' She quickened her steps as she reached the door. Carla stared after her, bewilderment increasing. It was beyond her comprehension how any two people could live under the same roof, share a bed and yet apparently have the spectre of murder between them.

Melvin left in a flurry of last minute orders, his attitude that of pleasurable excitement which he toned down to the level of business-like necessity. He shook hands with Carla and kept her hand in his a fraction longer than the occasion demanded. All that Carla was thinking about was the fact that it was unlikely she would be able to have dinner with Adrian, as planned, now that Vanessa would be alone. Almost as if by telepathy, Melvin said, 'I'm sure you can be spared for your dinner date – eh, Vanessa? Mustn't disappoint Adrian.'

The car moved away. There were tears in Vanessa's eyes as she and Carla returned to the house, but she brightened at the remembrance of the parcel. As she tore away the wrapping she talked quickly. She had ordered cuff links of special design, explaining how Melvin lost the first pair she had ever given him and was upset about it. Carla had the feeling that the observations were a kind of self hypnosis to wipe out the dark memories that otherwise would have driven her mad. Escaping into the past, concentrating on some concrete evidence of her own feelings, loyalties, took the razor edge off an almost unendurable suffering. The cardboard box revealed cotton wool and tissue paper.

'Not a very good way to pack things. They could at least have put them in a case.'

Carla agreed and then heard Vanessa's cry of astonishment as a diamond spray brooch dropped into her lap. Instantly, her face lit up. 'Oh, Carla! Isn't it *beautiful*. I've opened Melvin's parcel. I didn't take any notice of what was written. All I wanted to do was to hide it from him. This must be for my birthday...' She rummaged among the paper and looked at the address on the box. 'That's funny...'

'What's funny?' Carla asked, finding the poignancy of Vanessa's love like a personal hurt. One thought, one gesture and she could wipe out all the torture.

'It is addressed to me.' She continued, half talking to herself, 'Ah, here's a letter.' She began to read aloud:

'Dear Mrs Ingram,
We hasten to send on the brooch you left in your bedroom when you and your husband stayed with us last week.

It was a very great pleasure to have you with us again and we are looking forward to your visit next month. Your usual room, with bathroom, will be available.

Our kindest regards to you both.

Yours sincerely'

Vanessa's voice had become weaker and more puzzled with every word read.

'But this is ridiculous. They've got the wrong Ingram.' She stopped, her face suddenly drained of all colour. She echoed pitifully, *'You and your husband.* The hotel – Perth.'

Carla felt that someone had picked her up

and put her into a spin drier. It was all so obvious that any remark would be a travesty. She took refuge in anger, 'In any case for an hotel to send it back–' She stopped.

Vanessa sat dry eyed: 'They sent it back because they knew Melvin; because he was clever enough to give his right address and because they *know* them. "Your usual room, *with bathroom".'*

Carla got up and went to the cocktail cabinet, poured out a brandy and said, 'Drink this.'

Vanessa obeyed mechanically. Then she said dully, 'So now I know *why* he wants to murder me.' She shook her head to prevent Carla's interruption: 'He would never have the courage to be divorced – never... Funny, I'd never really thought of other women. Oh, I know men flirt and love flattery and that they're promiscuous. This is different. He must be very sure of things to identify himself with this – this *woman* and Polvose.'

'What do you mean?' Carla tried to remain calm and not to betray the fear which made her shudder.

'Can't you see? He must be very sure that the day is coming when Polvose *will* be their address. And he must have great faith in his prospective second wife,' she finished bitterly, tears gushing to her eyes. 'Men do not usually risk being friendly with the managers, or owners of hotels, when they are having just an affair. Oh, you can say that Perth is far away from here, but coincidence hardly respects distance.' Vanessa's expression was wild and tormented. 'Now I not only have the knowledge that he intends to kill me, but I know his reason for wishing to do so.'

Carla exclaimed rather desperately, 'You, also, are in a position to face him with the hotel letter.'

Vanessa gave a little moan, half despair, half resignation, 'If I were to do that he would crucify me.'

Carla said hotly, 'He's hardly the one to–'

Vanessa shook her head. 'You don't know Melvin – not at all. If I were to present him with the facts – indisputable facts – he would not say one word.'

Carla made a sound of angry disbelief.

'It's true, Carla. I've never known Melvin to admit anything, give a reason for anything, or really to say he's sorry. He withdraws behind a wall of silence, making you feel the guilty one.'

'But *this* – this is a vastly different thing.'

'I agree.' Vanessa's voice was flat and dead. 'But you haven't seen him in a rage and were you to do so once, you would never want to do so again.'

Carla thought of his anger the previous night, of the noise that filled the house threateningly. She waited a second wondering if Vanessa might refer to the episode, but no reference was forthcoming. Then she said, 'Rage and silence seem a strange combination.'

'The rage comes afterwards if anything touches upon a subject he either wishes to forget, or dislikes discussing. Now I know why he was so defensive when Adrian talked about his trips, or whatever he called them. No wonder, too, he was glad to have you here. Being with me alone must be sickening for him.' A sad, pitiful expression came into her eyes. 'I think I shall be glad to be put out of my misery. Nothing matters now.'

'Don't talk like that,' Carla said sharply.

'I wonder who she is.' Vanessa got up from her chair and paced the room. 'I expect he's with her now ... that telephone call ... the sudden going to Paris...'

'He had previously said he would probably be going,' Carla prompted, trying to cut through the suspicion.

Vanessa's half smile and the shake of her head was more eloquent than any words.

Carla felt trapped by an emotion she could neither define, nor fathom. Polvose was obviously a house to leave. This latest development added to the menace, and she knew that if her parents were aware of the truth they would beg her to return home. The thought of Adrian momentarily wiped out the problems around her and brought reassurance. She said swiftly, 'Isn't all this something that Adrian could deal with? He's your friend as well as Melvin's, after all.'

Vanessa hastened, 'I was going to ask you to tell him about the brooch and the letter.' As she spoke she picked up the flashing ornament, returned it to its tissue paper, put it – almost with precision – into the box and then did the box up in its original wrapping, using Sellotape which she took from her writing desk. The letter went into her handbag. 'The loss,' she said with faint cynicism, 'of the brooch will no doubt cause a little consternation. Perhaps I'm entitled to that small consolation.'

Carla agreed. 'And when they discover that the hotel sent it here?'

'No doubt Melvin will think up some plausible story as to why it was not received.'

'A registered parcel can always be traced,' Carla warned.

'When that happens, if I'm alive, I shall be quite ready to give it to him. But if I know Melvin nothing will be said. Who knows, it could be a weapon in my hands. To play the outraged wife would be horrible. I can hear his scorn… Will you talk to Adrian for me?'

'If you wish, but I cannot see how doing so will help.'

Vanessa said quietly, 'It will put him in the picture. In any emergency he would then be in possession of the facts. Don't look so anxious, this hasn't changed my feelings – only my attitude.'

Carla knew there was nothing more she could say. A little later they went into Fowey. It was a distraction if nothing else.

When Adrian telephoned that evening, Carla stressed that she would prefer to meet him, using her own car, rather than be called for at Polvose. The idea was Vanessa's. She was not in the mood even to see Adrian.

Carla found the restaurant which Adrian had suggested and felt that instead of driving a few miles she had crossed over to the continent. The tables were candle lit and gay with multi-coloured cloths. The atmosphere was discreetly romantic as though management and staff had conspired, in order that lovers might be the chosen guests. Almost immediately after sitting down at a corner table, their cocktails served, Carla felt a tingling sensation of excitement. Suddenly she and Adrian became two people involved with each other. Eyes looked into eyes with that intimacy of glance which defied description. After a while, Carla told Vanessa's story and as she finished, she was disconcerted by Adrian's attitude. There appeared to be neither surprise, nor condemnation, in his expression and when he spoke his voice was quiet to the point of reserve.

'I see,' he said, adding, 'I've never heard anything detrimental against Melvin.'

Carla bristled slightly. 'And how would you describe this?'

'Unfortunate.'

'Because he has been found out?'

'I was thinking of the effect on Vanessa,' he answered gravely.

Carla nodded understandingly. 'I cannot believe that to remain silent about it all will do any good.'

'And I wonder what would happen if Melvin were challenged. Vanessa must have some very good personal reason for not accusing him.'

Carla asked herself if Adrian fitted into the picture and was Vanessa protecting him. Had Melvin, in fact, the weapon to meet accusation with accusation? She said slowly, 'Is that a statement made in the light of knowledge, or merely an opinion?'

Adrian sipped his wine, avoiding her gaze, then, 'An opinion.' The momentary silence which followed his words was alien to their previous mood. Abruptly, almost suspiciously, he asked, 'Did you, by any chance, know Melvin before you came here?'

Carla stared at him aghast.

'Whatever makes you ask me that? Of course I did not know him. Had I done so I should have mentioned the fact. I must say I resent the question,' she finished hotly. Emotion forced her to add, 'And I would add that I could hardly have been in Perth and Polvose at the same time. If that is what you have in mind.'

'It wasn't,' he replied coolly, 'but if my memory serves me correctly, you and Melvin arrived at the house on the same day. He returning from Scotland and you coming down from Ascot. So you see how easy it is to build up any case.'

'And make two and two five.' Her eyes flashed, her cheeks flushed.

'You laid yourself open by your reference to Perth.' He smiled apologetically and with a whimsical amusement. 'Just the solicitor in me.'

'Then I hate the solicitor,' she flashed.

He looked at her intently, bringing back the excitement as he suggested quietly, 'But not the man, Carla.' There was no suggestion of conceit in the utterance which had a ring of inevitability.

'No,' she agreed honestly, 'not the man.'

They lingered over their wine, talking easily, exchanging views but not referring either to Melvin or Vanessa again, while each knew that the situation was fraught with danger and Carla had an instinctive feeling that Adrian was concealing facts which might have thrown light on the unusual circumstances. When their glasses were finally emptied and the candles had burned low, they went out into the cool still Cornish night, looking across the river to Polruan.

Lights, as though from fairyland, twinkled from cottages and the fishing boats and sailing craft lay at anchor, creating a scene of peace that yet promised excitement with the coming of a new day. Carla said involuntarily, 'It would be difficult to leave a place like this.'

Adrian looked down at her in the semi-darkness. 'Then I must make it not only difficult, but impossible, for you to do so.'

Carla laughed to cover her sudden nervousness. She was a little afraid of the man beside her and of his power to attract her. And although she would have liked him to enlarge on his statement, she felt a faint sense of relief because he remained silent. They walked to their respective cars and his manner was almost formal as he saw her into the driving seat and stood beside the open door, saying, 'I don't like the idea of your going back alone, but since it was your choice in the circumstances ... I'll probably call in at Polvose within a day or so.'

Carla sat with her hands on the steering wheel, looking up at him and trying not to betray the sudden sensation of deflation she was feeling. Her voice was smooth as she said, 'I'll tell Vanessa.'

'Meanwhile, should you need me you've only to ring.'

Carla murmured her thanks, disliking the fact that she wanted him to kiss her, while appreciating that she had hardly encouraged him to do so. She switched on the engine and put the car into gear. 'Thank you, Adrian, and for a delightful meal.'

His half smile told her nothing and she drove away. Her heart felt like an ice block. She was not aware of the journey back and when she had put the car in the garage, she began to wander restlessly towards the cliff walk. Vanessa had given her a key so that she could return to the house (now in darkness) at any time, so no one was being kept up on her behalf. Perhaps, she thought illogically, Adrian might have come by a different route and she might meet him as on the previous evening. Colour burned in her cheeks at her own folly. The narrow pathway was eerie and deserted, yet it drew her to it as though it had a secret to share. The silence appeared to deepen and was then broken by the faint sound of footsteps moving cautiously on the rough, stony surface. It wasn't possible that Adrian could have raced her back without his car being seen, yet the fugitive, fantastic hope persisted, only to die on the breath of fear as someone, in that second unrecognisable, paused as though alerted. She pressed back against the rock face, feeling sick with apprehension and then, as the figure turned, all the blood seemed to drain from her heart, leaving a terror greater than anything she had ever experienced in her life.

The man standing there was Melvin.

4

Carla recovered from the shock of Melvin's presence, because had she not done so she might have fainted and plunged to her death in the creek below. Survival became a stronger force than terror. She dare not move because her footsteps would be heard and if her presence was discovered then, she argued, she was quite prepared to face him with courage. Equally, she knew her own danger. He would not have gone to such lengths to leave for Paris (while intending to remain in the vicinity) unless he wished to keep the fact a secret. For what seemed to her to be hours and was merely a matter of seconds, he stood looking down into the well of darkness which the trees created. Then, having satisfied himself, so it seemed, that all was in order, he moved quietly in the opposite direction. Only then Carla thought of Vanessa. And the house in darkness. As in all moments of emergency and panic she had overlooked the obvious. Vanessa's safety. Now only that was important and she crept back as swiftly as silence would allow, let herself into the house – into the stuffy darkness which was alive with her own fear.

And as she groped for the light switch a hand closed over hers and Mrs Wells said softly, 'I'm sorry I turned all the lights out. I came down specially ... you're shaking.'

Carla knew she must keep her nerve. To break down now would be fatal. Obviously the woman was not telling the truth. Had she come down specially to light up the hall, she would not have done so without also illuminating the landing and staircase. Carla managed to keep her voice as steady as possible. 'A cold hand covering one's own in the darkness is enough to make anyone shake, Mrs Wells.' She could not keep the words back, as she added, 'Is everything all right?'

The dark figure moved away. 'Of course. Why do you ask?' The boot-button eyes might have been polished, they were so bright.

Carla ignored the remark, but relief overwhelmed her. For all that, she had the uncanny feeling that Mrs Wells had followed her every movement, from one window or another, since the car had been put in the garage.

'Can I get you anything? The nights are chilly ... hot milk?'

Carla thanked her and refused. As she reached the staircase, Mrs Wells said rather militantly, 'Mrs Ingram went to bed early. She had a slight headache.' The inference was that she should not be disturbed.

Once in her own room, Carla went to the window, having turned on only a bedside light. It seemed rather as though the world had died. No leaf stirred in the dark stillness outside. Melvin seemed to have vanished in space. But his ghost remained and she could find no answer to the question as to why he was there, unless for some sinister purpose. The perfect murder, planned with the precision of a military operation. She had no fear lest he had seen her and she began to wonder if she had been at fault not to confront him. Yet that would have given him the benefit of being forewarned. She remained at the window, watchful and alert. It was difficult to pick out any particular object, but just as she was about to turn away, she saw the flicker of a torch and caught a fleeting glimpse of a woman. It was quite impossible to determine her features and she disappeared as though sinking into the ground. Carla's foreboding increased. Did she fit into the picture with Melvin? An accessory?

A faint knock on the door renewed an earlier fear. Her voice was breathless as she said, 'Come in.' Overwhelming relief followed Vanessa's entrance, although it merged swiftly into anxiety. Vanessa was pale, trembling and almost dazed.

'I saw Melvin,' she said in a flat, defeated tone.

Carla felt that every nerve in her body had been charged with electricity. 'Melvin! But that's impossible.' She hoped her voice sounded convincing.

'I know.' Vanessa sat down on the edge of the bed, sagging like a rag doll. She stared around her without, Carla thought, anything registering. 'I must have had some kind of nightmare. But it was so real, Carla. He was there, in the room, looking down at me and I could feel his hatred.' She covered her face with her hands. 'Perhaps I'm going mad,' she added piteously. 'And I'm sorry to disturb you … did you have a happy evening?' The irrelevance added to the poignancy.

Had Melvin been in the house? Carla asked herself and the possibility created a new suspense. The great thing was to convince Vanessa that she had been dreaming. This, finally, she managed to do and then asked casually, 'Does Melvin ever telephone you when he is away?'

Vanessa shook her head. 'No, he hates the telephone and we're on a transfer service that enables us to bar all incoming calls. We can make outgoing ones.'

'Like a doctor transferring his number?' Carla was interested.

'I suppose so, only Melvin doesn't transfer to any other number. People who ring us just get the unobtainable note. We can do this as and when we like – I mean so far as the service is concerned.' She drew a hand across her forehead. 'Everything seems so mixed up and empty... I wonder what the woman is like – the woman he stayed with in Perth. I've thought of nothing else all the evening. I suppose that's why I had a nightmare.' She got up and pulled the sash of her tailored, blue satin house coat more tightly around her waist. 'I think I shall get dressed,' she exclaimed jerkily and defiantly, 'and go for a walk.'

Carla said with authority, 'You will do no such thing ... let's make some tea.'

Vanessa looked penetratingly at Carla and then turned her gaze to the window. 'Don't you trust me to be left up here alone – or to go out alone?'

'I just think,' Carla replied firmly, 'that there are times when we need someone to be with us – that's all.'

The moment that Carla and Vanessa opened the bedroom door and walked across the landing, Mrs Wells appeared. She was still dressed and might have been waiting for just that second. When Vanessa explained what she and Carla were about to do, the reply was instantaneous. 'I will make the tea and bring it to your room.' There was a slight emphasis on the word, 'your' and, with that, the solid black figure moved quickly down the stairs.

Vanessa thanked her. Carla asked, when

the two of them were back in Vanessa's room, 'Does she never go to sleep?' She infused a note of lightness. 'I'm sure she must go to bed fully dressed!'

Vanessa had a faraway look in her eyes. 'She's always alert when Melvin's away. I suppose she is when he's here, but it's different somehow. Yet she is so good to me. When you're very lonely – as I was until you came – that counts so much.'

Carla returned to her own room later on and instinctively went to the window. The night was so still that the scene might have been a painting. The trees were etched against the sky and their shadows were reflected mysteriously in the creek below. But in the woodlands to the right a small torch showed up like a star that had dropped from the heavens and could not find its way. Carla went to bed, determined that she would – for Vanessa's sake – confront Melvin if possible the following night. She had nothing to lose, or to gain, and she could return to Ascot at any moment she chose.

Return to Ascot… Leave Adrian. The thought was suddenly like a crushing weight on her heart.

The following night, when Vanessa was in bed, Carla cautiously left the house and made her way to the cliff walk. Melvin might, or might not, be in the vicinity, but she was determined to explore that mysterious part of the Polvose land. People could not vanish at the level of the tree tops without having some method, or pathway, of escape. The sound of footsteps alerted her and she stood still. Immediately there was silence. Obviously someone was exploring who did not wish to be seen. This time, she walked on, past the cavern which Adrian had pointed out and then moved along the hairpin bend ahead of it. There she came face to face with Melvin. For one paralysing second she knew terror. Any struggle and he could hurl her to her death in the creek below, without ever being suspect. But all he said was, 'You saw me here last night. I thought you would return tonight.'

'Why?' Carla clasped her hands tightly in an effort to stop trembling.

He lit a cigarette with calm, deliberate movements. 'Curiosity.' A faint smile played about his mouth. 'The finest place on earth to escape from everything is near one's own home.'

Carla wanted to say, 'Like the criminal hiding next to the police station,' but thought better of it. In fact her earlier plans seemed foolish, if not dangerous, as a possible protection for Vanessa. There was something rather deadly about Melvin as he stood there and she felt that no accusations would deter him from any line of conduct once he had made up his mind. 'It is rather fortunate that we all do not want to escape from everything.'

He puffed a tiny cloud of smoke into the air, his chin raised almost arrogantly. 'But we all have something we want to escape from. A job, a lover, a place. We deceive ourselves most of the time. Of course you can give me away. It will not really matter. I can't very well be charged with trespassing on my own land. I have my reasons for being here. I should forget having seen me if I were you. I have no wish to drag you into my affairs.'

The wind, suddenly getting up, seemed to echo mournfully through the trees, as though part of the tragedy ahead. Now, in the darkness, Carla's eyes were able to focus Melvin's and see in them a glint of steel. A faint, but unrecognisable sound, broke the silence that fell momentarily between them. And, concealed from their view – unable to overhear their conversation – Adrian watched. The fact that Melvin was at Polvose and Carla had met him at that late hour, renewed every suspicion and built up many more. Adrian recalled the occasion when he, himself, had met her wandering along that same walk, pretending that curiosity and concern for Vanessa were responsible. Her denial about having met Melvin before coming to Cornwall... It all built up to a point where his own anger and disgust made him feel physically sick. If only he could hear what they were saying, but he dare not move.

Carla wanted to escape almost as though she was in the presence of evil. Melvin's voice was more pleasant than his expression as he said, 'Just remember that you came to Polvose on account of my wife. I've never been very keen on watchdogs, but I prefer them to spies. For all that, I believe I can trust you.'

There was no way in which Carla could hit back without involving Vanessa, but she said firmly, 'I shall not betray you without warning you first that I intend to do so. Don't underestimate me as a watchdog.'

He laughed and to her amazement and annoyance, leaned forward and kissed her cheek. 'Good girl. I like a woman with spirit. And mind how you go back. This path could be dangerous.' With that he put a hand on her shoulder, turned, and was almost immediately lost to her view. She did not pretend to herself that she was not nervous, or that the situation did not fill her with fear. She began to walk, quickening her pace past the cavern as though scared of what it might reveal. If only Adrian was there to advise her. Her instinct was to get to him and tell him of all that had happened, but that was impossible and she made her way back to the house, and this time Mrs Wells did not disturb her.

Mrs Wells watched from her bedroom window. She knew all the secrets of Polvose and would have given her life in order to protect Vanessa from knowing the true facts.

To Carla's relief, Adrian called at Polvose the following evening. She had overcome her desire to telephone him, despite remembering his words, 'Should you need me, you have only to ring.' Was it that his manner had made her self-conscious? The feeling that he did not want to commit himself to any particular relationship, engendering half-formed fears and, as was the way of a woman, she recalled his words, yet again, when she had remarked – as she looked out on the Cornish scene – 'It would be difficult to leave a place like this.' It was useless to deny that his comment had not pleased her as he said, 'Then I must make it not only difficult, but impossible, for you to do so.' And seeing him, as he came into the house, she knew why she was there amid all the chaos and misery: because she was in love with him. Reason, common sense, had been her allies all her life but love had made nonsense of both, otherwise she would now be back and secure in her parents' house at Ascot, instead of living with the desperate fear, the suspicions and doubts, which clung to Polvose like cobwebs.

She went forward to greet him realising,

afterwards, that she had been like an eager child. All he asked was, 'Is Vanessa in?'

Carla looked, at that second, on a stranger. The tone of his voice, his manner, removed all warmth even from the remembrance of other hours. Yet he was not arch, or condescending. Politeness could be a far more bitter thing to bear.

'If you'll wait a second I'll get her,' Carla said, feeling gauche. 'You know your way around this house,' she added as she began to mount the stairs.

Adrian wandered into the study. He felt irritated and bad-tempered, wanting a whipping boy, while knowing that he was being immature in his reactions.

Vanessa welcomed him warmly, grateful for the distraction of his company. For a little while she could escape from her dark, suffocating and unhappy world. But after a few minutes she could not resist mentioning Melvin and looked from Carla to Adrian saying, 'Carla told you about Melvin, I know.'

'I'm so very sorry, Vanessa.' The words sounded flat and trite.

'You hadn't any idea?'

'None. And you haven't any idea of the woman's identity?'

Vanessa shook her head and then said almost defiantly, 'I don't want to find out either. I shall discover who she is one day,' she added darkly. 'She could live in the district – or even on this estate. I haven't seen half of all that Melvin owns.' She went on without continuity, 'It should be beautiful in Paris now ... we haven't been away together for three years... I must sound like a moaning wife.'

'Not without cause,' he said indignantly.

Carla listened, realising that Adrian's intonation, every shade of his expression became important to her and she told herself belligerently that if this was being in love, she preferred her former carefree, detached state. At the first opportunity, she escaped and went out into the garden.

Adrian joined her for a few minutes before driving away. 'I take it you haven't any idea which day Melvin is likely to be back,' he asked coolly.

Carla was grateful she could give an honest answer, even if out of context. 'Naturally I've no idea. Isn't it rather an odd thing to ask me?'

Adrian's gaze was speculative. He had hoped that she might confide in him and that his conclusions need not be right. 'I don't think so,' he replied. 'You could hardly have said anything in front of Vanessa.'

There was nothing that Carla could add. Her emotions were too tumultuous and she became a victim of them. She dare not resort to flippancy, or be provocative in case she should betray her own secret. She said quietly, 'No, I could hardly say anything in front of Vanessa.' And from that point no progress was possible. A hunger, which was a sick ache, started at the pit of her stomach. It was so new, so entirely unlike anything she had imagined, that words were lost in the dryness of her mouth which seemed to be filled with sawdust. Would he suggest seeing her again? Make any plans? But he said with a polite casualness, 'I'll ring Vanessa in case of any developments. She is quite adamant about keeping this business to herself.' He began to move slowly across the lawn towards his car. A fading light blessed the scene as though it had been filtered through a stained glass window. Vanessa came out and joined them, urging Adrian to stay for a meal. He refused, saying that he had work to do. Carla felt suddenly and intensely lonely, as he got into his car and drove away.

'Am I imagining things,' Vanessa said rather anxiously, 'or was Adrian strained – just something? When are you going to see him again?'

Carla longed for the courage to say, 'Never, because I'm going home tomorrow.' But, firstly, her love for him made that impossible and secondly, her affection for Vanessa had become very deep during the short while she had been at Polvose, and she knew that she could not desert her when most she needed protection. She tried to sound casual as she said, 'He probably has some worrying case on his mind... We didn't mention ourselves.' Her laughter was faintly nervous.

'Adrian is very attractive,' Vanessa said somewhat irrelevantly. Then she added with bitterness, 'And I used to delude myself that Melvin was jealous of him.' She turned her head abruptly. 'What was that noise? There's no wind, but those bushes – look! They're shaking.'

Carla could not deny the fact and she ran swiftly across the lawn. Was Melvin lurking in the grounds? Her search revealed nothing. 'Probably a rabbit, or a rat,' she said to Vanessa.

'A very tall rabbit, or rat,' Vanessa exclaimed. 'Those bushes are high and the top was moving.'

For some unaccountable reason, Carla said, 'Wells doesn't appear much – does he? Is that because Mrs Wells likes to be in charge?'

Vanessa's brows puckered. 'You weren't thinking that Wells was–'

'No,' Carla hastened, 'it was just an association of ideas...'

'Wells being tall.' Vanessa pondered the statement. 'He is dominated by his wife, but that doesn't matter so long as they look after us – does it?'

The telephone rang as they entered the

house. Vanessa answered it. *'Melvin!'*

Carla went from the room and returned when she heard the faint tinkle of the bell as the receiver was replaced.

'He's back in London – Melvin!' Vanessa spoke quickly and excitedly, but with an underlying note of suspicion. 'He's coming home, as he said, on Saturday night. Oh, Carla, if only things were different. Having to pretend – *pretend.*'

'I still think it might be better if you had all this out.'

'What is the good of starting something when you haven't the courage to fight?'

Carla looked grave as she said, 'Not even for your own life?'

'That least of all... Oh, I can be frightened, but not nearly so frightened as I should be of Melvin's rage if he found out I knew. He would taunt me with the fact that I hadn't the spirit to leave him and enjoy my misery without ever uttering a word of regret. I'm weak, Carla, and that is why I draw on your strength. You see, even being absolutely certain that Melvin intends to murder me ... well, the moment I heard his voice just now, my world lit up and all I could think about was that he was coming home.'

Carla nodded and understood. Then, suddenly, without quite knowing why, she remarked, 'A good thing you were on the telephone tonight.'

'I just had a feeling, I suppose. Hope, per-haps. I don't often go on transfer when he is away – just in case. Oddly enough, he didn't mention anything like that. He sounded almost pleased to hear me and long distance calls always seem so near.'

Carla dare not ask for any details such as if the operator spoke first. She would hate to pile suspicion on suspicion in Vanessa's mind, but she would have given a great deal to be certain that Melvin really was in Lon-don...

5

Carla awaited Melvin's return with appre-hension that Saturday night. She hated the idea of what might be a conspiracy between them in order to keep Vanessa from knowing the real facts. Could she have confided in Adrian, the whole situation would have fallen into proper perspective through his advice or guidance. In addition, she would have felt secure in, at least, a friendly rela-tionship. He had telephoned Vanessa during the intervening days and arranged to have a meal at Polvose that Saturday evening. He arrived before Melvin and Carla felt his gaze upon her with, what she felt to be, a suspicious scrutiny. His manner was withdrawn and subtly polite as on the previous occasion, while his attitude to Vanessa was charming and solicitous. Vanessa, despite the circumstances, looked particularly attractive and her plain white dress enhanced her fairness. Her eyes were full of eager anticipation and Carla marvelled at her ability to accept her position and still temper suffering with a bubble of happiness. She kept glancing at the clock, saying, 'Melvin should be here at seven, or just after.' Her voice had a note of high-pitched uncertainty which shattered the illusion created by her appearance, as though that bubble of happiness died before fear.

Adrian tried not to allow his preoccupation with Carla to be noticeable. He knew she was nervous by the movements of her hands and the way in which she was listening for the sound of an approaching car – listening while pretending not to do so. And at last Melvin arrived, Vanessa going out instantly to greet him. Just for those seconds, she told herself, that if she could be welcoming and loving, even then it might not be too late to save her own life and the marriage. Some childish faith burning brightly within her to give her courage.

Melvin kissed her cheek and said, 'I like the dress and the hair-do… I'm later than I intended. I see Adrian's here.' By that time

he and Vanessa had reached the sitting-
room and he added, 'A gathering of the
clans.' His gaze rested on Carla for a fraction of a second and he looked away quickly,
but not before Adrian had observed the
fact.

'Paris,' he exclaimed, 'was too hot for me.
Cornish air makes cities oppressive.'

Carla thought it was rather like a scene in
a play. The kind of thing people would
loftily dismiss as not being 'true to life' and
was just that. And equally unbearable.

'Then,' said Vanessa, 'you must have more
Cornish air.' Her voice trembled, despite
her effort to control it.

There was a rather smug look of satisfaction on Melvin's face as he replied, 'That
is just what I intend to have. I'm arranging
to get through a back-log of paper work.'
His smile was secretive. 'After all, I understand Carla is an expert secretary and I am
certain she will help me out.'

Adrian felt a sudden uncontrollable hatred
for Melvin that second. He wanted to lash
out and betray what he felt to be a tawdry,
miserable conspiracy. Only loyalty to Vanessa prevented his doing so. He said, somewhat cynically, 'I'm quite certain that Carla
will be more than delighted to give you a
hand.'

Carla shrank from the look Adrian flashed
in her direction as he spoke. She was at a

loss to understand it. All she could feel was a sick unhappiness and a renewed fear. Only Melvin was at ease, as he returned to his car and brought back two attractively wrapped parcels, handing one to Vanessa and the other to Carla. 'I could not leave Paris without some little gift for you both.'

Carla murmured a word of thanks, hating even the touch of the article which turned out to be an attractive compact. Vanessa produced a silk scarf in shades of blue and pink which, in different circumstances, would have delighted her. As it was she merely commented on the artistic pattern, and the ability of the French to be expert designers.

'Hardly enthusiasm,' Melvin suddenly rapped out, 'for my thought in buying it.' A certain peevish expression came into his eyes which was childish.

Vanessa cried, instantly fearful of his anger, 'I have always appreciated everything you've bought me.'

'That is most charming of you.' He laughed – a strangely taunting laugh which made Vanessa turn away so that no one should see the tears which gushed to her eyes. The tiny oasis of calm vanished, but she managed to overcome the emotion surging over her by saying, 'I think we'd all like a drink.'

'A very good idea,' Melvin agreed and

walked to the cocktail cabinet.

Adrian intercepted the glance which Melvin and Carla exchanged. It was impossible to assess its significance, but he realised that he hated the idea of any possible relationship between them and that jealousy whipped up his disapproval which further annoyed him. And suddenly, irrelevantly, he recalled his partner, Clark Faber's words, *'A sinister house filled with violence.'* Looking on the scene, knowing more about the people living in it, he had the uneasy feeling that there could well be truth in the statement. Yet the idea of violence appalled him. Had Carla brought this element into the atmosphere? Or was it that he, himself, knowing of Melvin's infidelity, was seeing everything out of proportion for no better reason than that he was forced to accept the possibility of Carla being the other woman? Melvin's decision to spend more time at Polvose lent strength to the belief. For security reasons, he knew very little about Melvin's job, except that it was exacting and had, thus far, taken him away from home a great deal. None of the facts – or apparent facts – satisfied his legalistic mind.

Once the drinks were poured out, Vanessa said, trying to sound bright, 'Ella and Paul want us to have dinner with them tomorrow.'

Melvin replied tersely, 'I thought you said

she had a baby–' He stopped, realising Adrian's gaze intently upon him.

Vanessa's voice was firm and defensive, 'Are you suggesting that she *hasn't* had one? – a boy, born the day Carla arrived here.'

Melvin looked awkward. 'Sorry, I've had a great deal on my mind recently. Nerves a bit on edge. Of course I remember, but surely it's early to be entertaining.'

Adrian laughed. 'You obviously don't know much about the way things are done these days!'

'True, thank heaven.' Melvin looked deeply into his glass as he added, 'I'm afraid tomorrow won't be any good to me.'

'But it's Sunday and it's ages since the four of us have got together.'

'Then a few more days won't really matter, will they, darling?'

'I accepted and–'

Melvin interrupted her, his voice smooth yet hurtful, 'Then you won't make the same mistake again, will you? I'm not in the mood to listen to a lot of drivel and ga-ga talk about babies. Nothing to stop your going.' He smiled as though he had won a great victory as he turned to Adrian and Carla. 'A very stubborn woman, my wife.'

Adrian's disgust found an outlet in the comment, 'I should use the word reasonable.'

There was a moment of dramatic silence when Carla held her breath in case of what might follow. Melvin smirked and looked pompous. '*You* do not live with her.' He paused, appeared to be about to add to the statement, thought better of it and went on as though nothing unusual had been said: 'Now how about a meal? I'm starving... Must wash.' At the door, he turned and addressed Vanessa. 'On second thoughts, we may as well go to the Fairbrights' tomorrow.' His expression was smug as he added, 'Just so long as we get back by nine-thirty.'

Neither Adrian nor Carla spoke as the door closed. Vanessa broke the silence with, 'Why nine-thirty? Unless it is in order to meet *her*... Adrian, would you pour me out another sherry?'

Adrian did as he was asked and, in addition, refilled Carla's glass and his own. He dare not trust himself to comment on Vanessa's remark, but was staggered by Melvin's behaviour which, unless he had witnessed it, he would hardly have believed. Even making allowances for nervous tension, such a display of flagrant bad taste made him want to walk out of the house and never return to it. He noticed that Carla avoided his gaze as he handed her the sherry. She looked, he thought, despite his anger, very lovely as she sat with the sun on her hair and face, emphasising the fine, clear skin and delicate features. Her dress was simple and the colour of pale jade. In some strange way he felt that she was a challenge. Certainly if she could tolerate Melvin – after his exhibition of a few moments ago – then it was incredible to him. As against that, might she not take it as a compliment to her, since Melvin had not wanted to go out the following evening. His retreat could be the measure of his discretion in the circumstances. All this made the situation a greater puzzle – the pieces without the pattern.

'Are you going out tomorrow evening?' he asked her suddenly and when Vanessa had left them alone together.

Carla felt the excitement of anticipation. She answered quietly, 'No.' When he made no comment, she added, 'Why do you ask?'

'I just wondered what you do here on your own.'

She stared at him in amazement. 'But I am never on my own – unless you call going for a walk, now and then, being on my own.'

He forced a laugh.

Carla, stung to indignation by disappointment, could not resist remarking, 'And if, with Mrs Wells here, you could ever be alone you would be very lucky.'

'Don't you care for her?' His tone was reasonable.

'I don't have to care for her.'

He nodded agreement. 'She is devoted to Vanessa.'

'I'm sure that is true. I just have a feeling

that she has a cine camera stored in the back of her head.' It was more than Carla intended to say, but emotion undermined discretion.

'Meaning that she is watchful, or suspicious – or both?' Adrian kept his gaze upon Carla's face with an unnerving intensity.

Carla did not want to pursue a conversation about Mrs Wells and she laughed as she said, 'Probably both! Just in case I run away with any of the silver. Anything can happen with a stranger in the house. She and I would always be strangers.'

'Odd, I've always found her as friendly as occasion demands.'

'It could be because you are male.'

'You evidently consider that an asset.'

'Depending on the male,' Carla retorted archly.

Melvin and Vanessa rejoined them in that second and they went into the dining-room for their meal. Melvin talked most of the time, because it was the best way of avoiding any questions. The fact did not escape Adrian's notice. Vanessa attempted to ask about Paris but was adroitly side-tracked. Nerves were taut and the atmosphere offered nothing soothing, particularly when Vanessa exclaimed, 'I thought I saw you standing beside my bed the other night, Melvin. It was so real that I just could not believe it was a dream.'

'And did you imagine that I was some

100

magician who could be in two places at once?'

Adrian tried to sound bantering. 'It would make an original case if a man were charged with breaking and entering his own house.'

Melvin's expression was inscrutable. 'Trust a lawyer to reduce it to legal terms! Heavens, how quiet and peaceful it is here. Paris gets noisier and noisier.'

'I'd like to hear the noise,' Vanessa said defensively, 'I never go away.'

'Then I must rectify that,' Melvin replied smoothly.

Vanessa shivered and glanced at Carla as if to say, 'That means for ever.'

It was an evening of tension, when conversation flagged and simple statements led to argument. Carla had never seen Melvin and Adrian so aggressive and she had to admit that the fault lay mostly with Adrian. Was it jealousy? The possibility stabbed her and she was thankful when the time to say good-night arrived. She was alone with Melvin for a matter of minutes while Vanessa talked to Adrian in the hall. Melvin inclined his head in their direction and said, 'My wife is a better actress than Adrian an actor. My return is not exactly popular with him.'

Carla, wretched, sick at heart, made no reply but went from the room and so to bed. That sound of Adrian's car in the stillness of the night seemed like a requiem to her hopes and yearnings. The memory of his kiss lingered to sharpen the edge of her unhappiness and she despised herself for not leaving Polvose, but some force stronger than reason kept her there.

When Melvin and Vanessa left the house to go to the Fairbrights' the following evening, Carla set off, determined to discover the whereabouts of Melvin's hideaway. Somewhere, she told herself, there was a cottage that he visited and at which he had no doubt been staying the past few days. Equally, the woman she had glimpsed must fit into the picture somewhere. She wanted to strike from strength should it ever be necessary, for she was in no doubt of Melvin's cunning should he wish to incriminate Adrian. Intuition told her that while Adrian might be in love with Vanessa, she was not in love with him. He might be a dear friend, but not a lover.

The cliff walk held no terrors as she reached it, for the sun poured down on the panorama of sea, river and wooded hills, giving the scene a majesty which, in a second of contemplation, recalled to her mind lines written by Sir Arthur Quiller-Couch: *While the tides flow up and down the Fowey River, youth will be happy on its banks and, returning beneath the woods where Tristram and Iseult were lovers two thousand years ago, there will still be the old echo for Challenge by Wiseman's Stone and still at the turn, there will be riding lights and tomorrow the horizon, the open sea and adventure for youth.*

Carla felt a surge of emotion which seemed to identify her with the richness of the history around her. And upon it all was superimposed her love for Adrian which, despite being unrequited, nevertheless absorbed all her thoughts and etched a new design for living. Every leaf on every tree quivered in its reflected glory and, wherever she looked, it was his face she saw and every sound merged into the echo of his voice. And just as the view was illimitable, so was the dimension of her passionate need. One of those incomprehensible moments, when the heart and soul reached out to infinity.

Having slackened her pace, she quickened it again, impatient of her own emotionalism. When she reached what had always seemed to be the end of the walk, she stopped, baffled and momentarily defeated. Only rock face loomed ahead like some giant door covered, here and there, with greenery. It was only when she had stared and prodded with a branch broken from a tree at the start of her journey, that she realised the obstacle before her was not as solid as it appeared. Carefully moving aside the overhanging leaves and trailing fronds, a roughly con-trived door became visible. And it opened to her touch. A shiver of excitement went over her. For there ahead was a sloping, rubble pathway and while it was dark, nevertheless a shaft of light poured through it from a distant outlet. She hesitated, looked back to make certain she had not been followed and then set about re-arranging the foliage over the door, while leaving the smallest opening through which she could squeeze. Once inside she found she could stand upright as though in some vast tunnel which she could well imagine being used by smugglers in any age. There was the smell of damp earth, the tang of the sea and strange moss-like plants. The air was cold and the wind came to her in gusts as she neared the outlet which dipped into woodland far below the spot from which she started. Fear came at her sickeningly in that second of realisation that she would have to retrace her steps. She stood shaking; mentally planning the area around her. The blue waters of the creek seemed like fluttering lace against the trees. It was a scene of magic as the sun danced, like flickering golden shadows, elusive and tantalising, about her. For all that, it was wild and uninhabited. Melvin's land and his retreat. She managed to ease herself down a steep pathway which brought the creek nearer, and suddenly caught a glimpse of a low stone wall which brought her finally to a concealed building which had the appearance of a lodge. So this was the answer. Even before entering it, she felt the atmosphere of a place lived in and even well kept. A heavy, gnarled oak door offered no admittance and she crept stealthily around to the back, where an ancient octagonal archway led to a flagged portico which must have been hewn out of some previously submerged ruin.

The silence was broken only by the screeching of gulls as they wheeled overhead. A breeze from river and sea chilled the air and she drew her cardigan more closely about her. A latch-type door gave a breath of hope. It might lift to her touch, but when it did she gave a cry of fear at her own daring. Breaking into strange hideaways was not her forte. For all that, she squared her shoulders and stepped inside. And in that second she knew she was not there alone. Every pore of her skin seemed to be electrified as a voice – coming from a direction she could not exactly place – said, 'I'm so sorry to be the wrong man.'

'Adrian,' she gasped as he came towards her from an adjoining room.

His expression was cynical. 'Now I know why you did not tell me that Melvin was not in Paris, but in the district.' His gaze was withering. 'I congratulate you both on a perfect deception.' Before Carla could reply he added swiftly, 'Or are you going to deny that you knew he was here?'

Carla was so shocked, so shaken and so

furious, that she cried, 'I am not going to deny anything since you have already made up your mind about the situation. And, in any case, what business is it of yours?' Even as she uttered the words they hurt her.

'My concern,' he replied icily, 'is Vanessa. Your actions are certainly no concern of mine: her welfare is. She has been through enough without have to discover that you – you, of all people – are the woman in the picture.' He paused significantly before saying scathingly, 'I always suspected that you had known Melvin before you came here. At least I am now sure of my facts. You're in love with him and–'

'As you are in love with his wife.' Carla's voice was cold and contemptuous.

They faced each other in quivering hostility. Adrian had never been so angry. His face was white, his lips pursed. Then, with deadly calm, he said, 'If it suits you to believe that in order to excuse yourself, do so by all means. And just in case you should think up any more lies, I saw you and Melvin together the other night on the cliff walk *and* the touching little farewell scene.'

Carla put a hand up to her mouth to stifle her cry. Icy fingers touched her heart, as she recalled the unaccounted-for noise on that occasion.

'I thought that would refresh your memory.'

She shook her head. 'But you don't under-stand.'

'No.' His gaze was like a ray cutting into her heart. 'Then why are you here?' As he spoke he glanced around the room which was sparsely, but artistically, furnished. The embers of a recently lit fire remained in a large stone fireplace. Two glasses stood on a tray on a small table. Brandy, whisky and various other drinks, took up most of the top of a miniature cabinet. A woman's cardigan lay carelessly on the arm of a chair. Adrian walked to a door leading off the room and flung it open. It was a bedroom, reasonably tidy and on the dressing-table stood all the cosmetics any woman could desire. The frag-rance wafted to them and Adrian slammed the door almost violently. Carla accepted it as a gesture of envy. She knew, without doubt, that Vanessa was not in love with him, but the fleeting thought was lost in her own misery. She began urgently, 'Adrian, please listen; there is so much I would like to tell you.'

He looked at her and was suddenly quiet, almost detached. When he spoke he might have been addressing a stranger. 'And noth-ing I wish to hear – nothing I would believe.'

With that he turned and walked out of the cottage.

Carla flopped down in the nearest chair. She felt physically sick and desperate, because emotion had robbed her of the power to say any of the right things. Yet, on the face of it, her presence there was damning evidence and since Adrian had seen her with Melvin, every word she uttered in defence would seem hypocritical. Now she knew why he had treated her with such indifference, behaved as though there had never been anything more than mere politeness between them. Colour rushed to her face because her reflections suddenly seemed so naïve. What had there been between them except a brief flirtation? And where it had pleased him and acted as a palliative, now the possibility that she might endanger Vanessa's happiness changed the picture entirely and awakened his fury and scorn. In truth, he could be no more content with his life than she, Carla, was with hers.

Looking around the room she felt an intruder. This must represent Elysium to Melvin since he made such elaborate plans to reach it. She could imagine his charm, even his being a good lover. But why did he remain with Vanessa? The answer seemed to leap out of the lengthening shadows: *In order to murder her.* Murder would seem far more dramatic than everyday divorce, and without its attendant discomforts. The more she dwelt on the possibility, the more convinced she became that Vanessa was not romancing, or trying to build up a situation out of the figment of her imagination. She remained sagging in her chair, for a few more moments. The thought of the journey back no longer scared her; emotion had turned its dark shadow to unimportant shades of grey. It was just as she got to her feet that the latch on the outer door clicked up. Her heart quickened its beat in an eager hope. Adrian might have come back. But she knew in a second that this was not so, and that whoever was about to come into the room was light of tread and female as a faint fragrance preceded her. Carla nerved herself to move forward at the moment when a slender figure cried, 'What are you doing here?'

And as she spoke she untied her head scarf to reveal dark curly hair. There was fire in her eyes and war in her attitude as she repeated the question – this time more aggressively.

Carla felt suddenly calm as she answered, 'Who are you?'

There was a moment of electric silence, then, 'It so happens that I live here.'

Carla studied the rather interesting, high-cheek-boned face, the small nose and well-shaped mouth. But the expression concealed fear. Fear that made her gaze dart from point to point in the room as though to assure herself that everything was as she had left it. She also looked at her wrist watch with faint apprehension before adding, 'You're trespassing. I don't like strangers.'

'So,' Carla said smoothly, 'you live here.'

'That's what I said. Any law against it?' And all the time she was watching Carla with suspicion. 'How did you find your way?' Now, her voice was unsteady and she burst out, 'No one knows the way here – no one,' she finished vehemently. 'Get out – get out.' Restraint vanished, the earlier attempt at control no more than a feeble hope of achievement.

Carla noticed that she wore a wedding ring and a slender gold chain around her neck on which hung a locket. 'I live,' Carla said deliberately, 'at Polvose. You may know Mr and Mrs Ingram.' She hastened, 'I'm Carla Selby.'

The slender figure appeared to droop like a sack in a nearby chair.

'So you *know*.'

'Some things – yes.'

'Please forget about this – *please*.' The arrogance, the challenge, had gone and, in its place, was an almost pathetic appeal. 'You must have had some reason for coming here – even attempting to find it – but only tragedy–'

Carla interrupted, the word *tragedy* building up her mounting fears. 'Isn't tragedy rather a dramatic word?'

'There isn't a dramatic enough word to cover all that I mean.' The dark head moved from side to side. 'And I thought we were safe here. Why – *why*,' she asked, her voice rising, 'did you come?'

Carla told her without prevarication.

'And now you will tell *her*.' The words sounded like a requiem. 'There has been peace – peace.'

Something about the girl awakened sympathy, even compassion, as Carla watched and listened. Did she know anything about Perth, or was that another escapade of Melvin's – another affair? Somehow she could not pry and had no desire to wound. Neither would serve any good purpose so far as Vanessa was concerned. Carla said quietly, 'You misjudge me, yet you knew my name.'

'I – I was told about you. I'm Gina Clements. You might just as well know.'

Carla commented, 'My concern is for Mrs Ingram. But that doesn't mean I would hurt her because of any discovery I might have made in connection with her husband.'

Gina Clements flinched at the sound of the word, *husband*. She looked very young and curiously untouched as she got to her feet. She threaded her fingers through the soft dark curls that lay almost childishly on her forehead. 'I have to keep it short so that I can wash it myself,' she explained incongruously, and as though she appreciated that Carla would understand her isolation. She rushed

111

on irrelevantly, meeting Carla's gaze with what appeared to be honesty, 'I suppose I always knew that one day someone would find this place, and when I heard about you and saw you here just now ... I felt certain you were from Polvose. Polvose,' she repeated, 'how I detest that name and everything it stands for.' Her eyes gleamed with a strange fire. 'But one day everything will be changed. Everything. I've been grateful for you – you might just as well know. There's been more freedom – to talk and to plan. If I could trust you not to mention this place or me–' She paused hopefully.

Carla said firmly, 'You can trust me. My loyalty is to Mrs Ingram, and as I've already said, I've no intention of hurting her.' She finished with telling emphasis, 'But in your circumstances I should think twice about trusting a man who hid me away in a place like this.' Carla waited tensed for the comment which, when it came sent a shudder over her.

'Only death can give you my reasons.' The words were spoken quietly and with an inevitability which made them a knell.

Carla felt that an icy wind lowered the temperature of the room in which they stood. The trees around them which had seemed so still, suddenly trembled, their branches swaying to and fro. Carla managed to ask, although scared of betraying the tumult within her, 'Why death?'

Gina Clements went to the window, her back towards Carla. 'Death reveals all secrets.' She added, 'Sooner or later.' She turned. 'Don't come here again.' There was a note of warning in her voice, a change of mood, 'And if you want to get back to the morgue unseen, you'd better go quickly.'

Carla left, her legs shaking, her heart thumping as she began the climb back to the tunnel. She knew instinctively that danger lurked no matter in which direction she looked. And now there was not even Adrian to whom she could turn for understanding, or support. The meeting with Gina Clements had an element of fantasy interwoven in its dramatic pattern. Concentration on it enabled her to reach the outlet of the tunnel without panic, except for that second of relief when she had gained freedom – a second of paralysing, delayed shock. Meticulously she replaced the greenery and marvelled, anew, at the dexterity with which an opening had been hewn, originally, out of the rock face. In this, no doubt, she argued, smugglers had done the greater part of Melvin's job for him. The light was fading from the evening sky, its muted glow giving an almost unearthly beauty. Every tree appeared to be brushed with gold dust and the peace of Sunday lay upon the land.

Carla hurried back to the house and went

straight to her room. As she did so, she heard the telephone ring. For the first time no emotion stirred within her. It would not be Adrian.

But as Mrs Wells answered it, Adrian said, 'Please can I speak to Miss Selby?' At the back of his mind there was a fugitive hope that Carla might have returned and that he had been unjust. Yet he was at a loss to understand the tumult and conflict within him.

Mrs Wells' voice was soft and sibilant as she said, 'I'm sorry, Mr Grant, but Miss Selby went out some time ago and has not returned.' She added pleasantly, 'Can I take a message?'

Adrian endeavoured to keep the anger from his voice. 'No message, thank you, Mrs Wells.'

Mrs Wells replaced the receiver with a gesture of triumph, but as she looked up and turned away, her husband stood glaring down at her.

'You watched her come back,' he said harshly. 'You know she is in the house. I've a good mind to tell her.'

The beady eyes flashed a warning. 'Do that and we'll find ourselves without a home, or a job. We're too old to begin again.'

He replied sadly, 'And you could not bear to be parted from her. You hate the idea of Miss Selby being anywhere near her...'

6

Carla lay awake that night in a world of distortion, her worries, her emotions, taking ominous shape. In the semi-darkness, even the furniture loomed menacingly. She would go back to her parents. Why should she be caught up in this world of mystery and misery? Yes, that was what she would do and tell Vanessa in the morning. So she loved Adrian, but so many people had loved and forgotten – she would join the procession. *Polvose*, a dreary place anyway. Isolated. What did it matter that she had met Gina Clements, or that she had found Melvin's sanctuary? Back to Ascot and normality! That was it. Then there was Mrs Wells always snooping around and jealous of her friendship with Vanessa. Adrian thought that she was Melvin's mistress. Let him think so – it no longer mattered, because she had made up her mind. This was a gloomy house waiting for murder.

Well! She would read about it in the news-papers. Because she liked Vanessa and was sorry for her, was no reason why she should ruin her own life and be as miserable as she was now. As for Adrian! She would forget

115

him the moment another man came into the picture. But what seemed to be a slab of concrete crushing her heart remained until she drifted into sleep.

Morning came and with it, normality. The sun streamed into the room and Carla drank her morning tea (which Mrs Wells had brought, as usual, but on this occasion, with a pleasantness that made Carla suspicious). All the memories of the previous evening came back with the impact that follows oblivion. Rather like going to the theatre, or cinema, and forgetting the problems, the tragedies, until that moment when either the curtain comes down, or The End appears on the screen and the heart and mind are once again tuned in to reality.

Carla tried to make normality reality. The two things were one, and yet in strange juxtaposition. Everything she had thought before going to sleep appeared to be a true assessment. Now, only Adrian dominated her thoughts. She knew herself well enough to accept the fact that she was neither facile, nor promiscuous. Did that make her a fool? It was impossible for her to answer her own question. She had known so many people who were both, and extremely happy. That brought her to Vanessa. And before she had analysed her thoughts, Vanessa came into the room. She began without preliminaries, 'It was a dreadful evening. I didn't like to dis-

116

turb you when we came in.'

Immediately, Carla became involved again. 'What do you mean by a dreadful evening?'

Vanessa sat down in an armchair by the window. Her fine blonde hair framed itself around her face in fluffy disorder. Without any make-up, her skin had the transparency of cellophane smoothed over white paper. 'Melvin hated every second of it. All he cared about was getting away. He loathed the baby – and it cried.'

Carla said, instinctively maternal, 'Babies do cry.' She added, 'So do grown ups, only they avoid making so much noise.' And all the time she talked, she was saying to herself, 'Tell her you are going. Get out of this misery before it is too late.'

She tried to frame the right words, while watching Vanessa, whose hands had dropped into her lap as though all strength had gone from them. Suddenly, Carla found the courage to say, 'Vanessa, I just cannot stay here.' The words seemed to swirl round the room and be amplified by some loud speaker.

The silence that followed was unbearable – as though the room had become a tomb.

Vanessa moved and sat on the edge of Carla's bed. 'I knew you were going to say that. In your place I should feel the same.' And even as she spoke, she lowered her head and cupped her face in her hands, tears rolling down her cheeks. Then, with courage and dignity, she squared her shoulders and said, 'Thank you for your patience. I could not have found anyone who understood as you have done.'

A knife seemed to penetrate Carla's heart. She put out her hand, incapable of any discussion, but knowing that, after all, this was something she must see through to the end. Just then, not even Adrian was important.

'I'm sorry,' she murmured, 'please believe me. I cannot go. In unhappiness, people become very close.'

Vanessa clutched and hung on to the outstretched hand and with a muffled, 'Bless you, Carla,' went from the room.

Downstairs, Melvin sat opening his letters far earlier than was his custom. Being a meticulous man, he immediately noticed a Perth postmark and every nerve in his body seemed electrified.

The letter read:

Dear Mr Ingram,
We may be unduly concerned , but we returned a brooch left by your wife on your last visit and not having received any acknowledgment are uneasy in case it might have gone astray. Hoping you and Mrs Ingram are well—

Melvin stared at the words as though they had taken shape as ghosts. They could mean only that the brooch had been returned to

118

Polvose, in which case Vanessa must have it. And he thought he had been so clever always to give his right address, because the distance between Perth and Fowey was great. Together with the fact that the years had lent security. Also, he was afraid of building up a situation that might explode in his face. He *did* live at Polvose and he had a wife whom he would never take to Perth – any more than she would wish to go. He reduced the situation to cold, clinical deduction. He could assume that the brooch had been registered. It was also vital that he find it. Only Vanessa could have it. At that point fury leapt within him like flames rising from a fire. Why, then, had she not accused him of his infidelity? The word jarred. Blast the damned hotel people for being such fools. *Fools!* Yet had he not gone out of his way to build up the picture of a perfect marriage – to talk of Polvose – in fact to project his own desires so that he was spared the indignity of being just an unfaithful husband whose name was entered in an hotel register? A breath of justice touched him. The owners of that hotel could not be faulted because of his own stupidity.

He sat there motionless. Wells, coming into the room to put the finishing touches to the breakfast table, asked anxiously, 'Sir, are you all right?'

'Perfectly all right, Wells. Just day dreaming.' A sinister, sadistic gleam lay just behind his half smile. Once all this was over, life would be very different. *Very* different. 'Breakfast ready?'

'Yes, sir. Madam and Miss Selby are just coming down the stairs. A lovely morning.'

'Lovely,' Melvin agreed, thinking that he must get through to the hotel and discreetly smooth matters out.

Wells, observant, intuitive, knew that the master was not in the best of moods. It did not worry him; he was used to them all.

Melvin slipped the letter into his pocket, thinking of Mrs Wells, who always attended to the post. Even if she studied the envelopes, his trips to Perth had never been a secret, and his job gave him an infallible excuse. Anger flared anew. For the brooch to have been left at the hotel in the first place was inexcusable. No fault of his. And why should he be forced to give a false name or address, just because he was staying with the woman he loved, instead of the woman he had married? By this time he had restored the greater part of his confidence and self esteem. But it would need discretion in handling the hotel problem, particularly as the owners, Arthur and Renie Warne, had always been in such friendly association with him.

Vanessa and Carla came into the room at that moment. Vanessa said – more because

120

of nervous tension than anything else – 'Not often you look at the post as early as this.' As she spoke she glanced at the five or six letters, already opened, that lay on a small table by his chair.

His expression changed. 'You have missed your vocation, my dear.' There was an underlying note of contempt in his voice.

'How?' The sick sensation of deflation returned.

'Private detective.' He looked from face to face. 'Come to think of it, that could apply to you both.'

Vanessa ignored the comment.

'There are no letters for you,' he said. 'Your friends are neglecting you.'

They were seated at the table by this time. Melvin felt that his thoughts must be noisy. He wanted to get both women out of the house and said suddenly and with an incredible change of manner, 'Now why don't you two have a day out? Get Mrs Wells to make you up one of her special picnic lunches. I've a great deal of work to do and shall put the telephone on transfer so that no one disturbs me.'

Vanessa was torn between wanting his company, while dreading any scenes that might result.

Carla looked at Melvin very directly. 'Are you sure you do not need any secretarial help?'

'Quite sure; but thank you for the thought.'
He had a second helping of scrambled egg and another rasher of bacon, followed by two slices of toast and marmalade. 'I shall have a light lunch and then break off for an hour or so, go for a walk and return to more work.'

Vanessa watched him carefully. It was painful to know any other human being quite so well as she knew him, or to be able to judge his motives so accurately. He might do a little work, but he wanted the house to himself and was prepared to be pleasant in order to achieve his own ends. Thwarting him would renew either contempt, or fury. He added brightly, 'How about a cinema this evening? We could run into St Austell.' Her impulse was to say, 'But you hate the cinema,' but prevented herself in time, instead suggesting: 'It's an idea. We can decide later on.'

'Splendid.' There was a suppressed excitement about him – characteristic of him when getting his own way. 'Take Carla to St Mawes,' he said, his speech quickening. 'Show her the round castle and don't forget to remind her that traders from the Mediterranean came there before Julius Caesar had set foot on our shores.' He laughed gaily.

Vanessa felt the ache of longing for happiness and she said swiftly, hoping that she might take advantage of his mood,

'Could you not come with us and tell her yourself? You know so much about the history of Cornwall.'

Melvin's eyes seemed to be as large and dark as black grapes standing out in a suddenly paling face. Carla knew that his temper was about to blaze and dreaded the possibility. To her relief, he smiled at Vanessa and remarked indulgently, 'You go on your own today, and we'll arrange something later in the week.' He got up from the table after the manner of a bustling business man late for an appointment. At the door he turned and fixed his gaze upon Vanessa. 'What time do you want to get away?'

Vanessa's answer was spoken lifelessly. 'About eleven.'

Melvin went out into the garden and returned to the sitting-room, where Vanessa and Carla were having coffee before leaving. He was cheerful and pleasant. 'Ah, coffee! Good.' He observed with satisfaction that the two women were prepared to go out.

Vanessa studied him overtly as she poured out his coffee. He took the cup from her and drank standing up. He didn't want them to linger so that he had to indulge any fatuous conversation.

And at last they left. 'Now don't hurry back,' he said, having seen them into the car and noticing, gratefully, that the picnic basket was on the back seat.

The car went off. He watched it until it was out of sight and then hurried into the house. Mrs Wells came forward. 'Your study is ready for you, sir.'

'*Ready* for me,' he repeated. 'Isn't it always ready?'

Her beady eyes met his without expression. 'We always turn it out on a Monday, because you are rarely at home on that day.'

He ignored that, saying, 'I'm not feeling too well. I shall lie down for a while. I don't want to be disturbed.' With that he left her and put a call through to Perth.

Arthur Warne was obviously pleased to hear him. Melvin thanked him for his letter and then allowed him to do the talking, so that he was not placed in the invidious position of asking questions. 'You see,' Arthur Warne explained: 'since naturally the parcel was registered, we did not want to start slanging the postal authorities, without being sure of our facts. Knowing your wife as we do, we became anxious at not hearing. So we thought the best thing was to drop you a line.'

'Perfectly right,' Melvin said stoutly, his heart feeling that it had dropped inches in a matter of seconds. 'I think the explanation is that she has a great friend staying with her and you know what it is when two women get together – everything goes by the board. I shall have to take her to task.'

The remark brought forth laughter and the request on no account to do so, also how much everyone at the hotel was looking forward to their forthcoming visit. On that note the conversation ended. Melvin considered it would be indiscreet, at that stage, to cancel the booking. He had not actually said that the brooch *had* been received, but he forestalled inquiries about it – without putting anything in writing.

The question was: who had the brooch? He could not have made an issue of it, so far as Arthur Warne was concerned, without telling him the truth. Could he ask Mrs Wells if she recalled a registered parcel being delivered just about the time that Miss Selby came to live at Polvose? He pondered the matter. It was against his rules to allow an employee to know anything about his personal affairs. But wasn't this rather different? Who paid the woman, his thoughts raced on angrily, and if he could not ask a simple question... But how simple was it? She would have signed for any registered package and, in that case, would know for whom it was intended and to whom she gave it. Would his inquiries arouse suspicion? 'Suspicion,' he said aloud, 'be damned.' There were many reasons why it was essential for him to know at least some of the truth about all this. The decision made, he flung open the bedroom door and went down the stairs like a cyclone, steadying himself just before he reached the hall. There he rang the bell which Mrs Wells answered.

Melvin not only tried, but succeeded, in sounding matter of fact.

'Mrs Wells, I wonder if you could help me … do you recall having signed for a registered package recently?' He watched that impassive face intently.

'Why, yes, sir.' There was no hesitation, or apparent cunning, in her manner. 'I remember because our usual postman was ill and the new man grumbled about finding the house. Also it was very soon – I couldn't rightly say what day – after Miss Selby came here.' She added truthfully, 'I was expecting it, if I'm not giving any secrets away.'

Melvin hoped he did not look as ill as he felt. His smile seemed to him to be like cracking parchment because the muscles of his face appeared to be paralysed.

'Really. Why?'

'Something that Madam had ordered on appro.' She smiled benignly. 'You have a birthday every year, you know.'

Melvin pretended to relax. 'And that is the only registered parcel delivered here recently?'

'Oh, yes, sir. I hope there's nothing wrong.'

'Only,' Melvin said with what he considered to be inspiration, 'that someone in my department has failed to carry out orders and send me information for which I asked. Thank you, Mrs Wells.'

'I'm sorry, sir. I signed for a small package and Miss Selby took it to Madam. I believe it was the day you went to Paris – *that* was it. Miss Selby helped a great deal that day.'

And Miss Selby took it to Madam.

Melvin managed to say: 'I appreciate birthday presents, Mrs Wells, but not inefficiency where my staff is concerned. Of course registered packets have been known to go astray and that is my worry.'

Mrs Wells inclined her head in understanding, but she said subtly, 'That is true – but not once they reach Polvose.' Her voice rose anxiously, as she added, 'I know you will not say anything to Madam. I ought not to have given her secret away.' She eyed him with concern. 'I hope your headache is better.'

'I'm afraid not. I'll rest a little longer.' He returned to the bedroom. Where to find the brooch? And how much did Carla know about it and how far was she responsible for Vanessa's silence? It was as though everything was closing in on him, making the house alive with his own hatred.

He locked the door and stood looking helplessly round him. Where to start the search? Vanessa's bureau provided the answer. Somewhere in it, there was a secret

127

drawer. He remembered her mentioning the fact and laughing about the little mementoes kept there. He even recalled how the idea bored him.

The flap of the bureau was unlocked and he pulled it down. His hands, delicate of touch, travelled over the drawers and compartments as a blind man's hands might travel over Braille. Perspiration stood on his forehead, but his expression was grim and determined as he refused to be beaten. And at last, suddenly, a compartment shot open. Inside, wrapped in tissue paper, was the brooch which he grasped urgently. Then he fumbled for the letter. Arthur Warne would obviously have enclosed a covering letter which might well be a greater indictment than the brooch itself.

The possibility that Carla might have the letter struck him. The two women were in league and he had no doubt whatsoever that Vanessa would have confided in Carla.

He searched both rooms, meticulously – cupboards, bags – every available receptacle. To no avail. He realised that in any emergency he would be doubly condemned. Finally, he looked down at the brooch and sank into a chair near the window in Carla's room. On no account must he precipitate a crisis. He would return the brooch and recover it in his own time. The concern about the letter increased, but he did not discount the possibility of Vanessa destroying it. At this point his vanity was greater than his fear. If any wife could keep quiet about the brooch, he reasoned, she could also destroy the letter that accompanied it. Her one aim was to preserve her marriage. The thought appealed to him. He got up, drawn to the partly open window which held the sinister fascination of destruction and with it, the ecstasy of fulfilment.

He returned the brooch to its hiding place and when he left the room, looked carefully about him. Why should he trust Wells – or his wife? They could be in league with Carla. Vanessa had been protected all her life, why should Carla be any different? After all, she had kept quiet about his being in Cornwall, when he was supposed to be in Paris. Could he fault her?

The landing, as he stood, looking around him, was as quiet as an empty museum, until Mrs Wells said, glancing up at him from the hall: 'Can I serve your lunch now, sir? Or would you prefer coffee and sandwiches?'

Melvin straightened his back and moved down the stairs with military precision. When he reached the hall, he answered: 'No thank you. I need some fresh air and, when I return, I would enjoy a cup of tea and some of your excellent sandwiches.'

'And should anyone telephone?'

Melvin looked at her with sudden interest.

Her eyes, he decided, might be like those of a large teddy bear. They could have been stuck in her face, as an ornament in pastry.

His voice was crisp and authoritative. 'Take their number and tell them I will ring them back.'

With that he walked to the front door and vanished into the sunlight which, at that point, made him lost in shadow.

The smile on the face of Mrs Wells was as inscrutable as that of the Mona Lisa.

7

When Carla turned out of the drive of Polvose, Vanessa said, 'I don't want to go to St Mawes, I want to go into St Austell.'

Carla braked automatically. 'Why?'

'I want to see Adrian.'

Carla sat tensed at the wheel of the car. 'You will have to tell me the road signs.'

Vanessa directed her through Fowey, Par, on to the Plymouth Road, past the Britannia Inn and Nettles Corner – a house as well as a bus stop – then straight through Holm-wood, Mount Charles and into St Austell.

'Adrian's offices are not far from the Post Office,' Vanessa said. 'If you park by the Church and the brewery–'

They laughed for the first time.

'A good combination,' Carla chuckled, turning up a Cornish gradient and parking on the side of a small mountain. For a second the knowledge that she was going to see Adrian brought happiness which was like sun, streaming through cloud, on a dark winter day.

Vanessa might not have heard her. As they got out of the car, she pointed to Fore Street and The White Hart. 'We'll have lunch there,' she said, with a quiet inevitability which made Carla instantly sad.

'But we brought a picnic basket!'

Vanessa nodded. 'I did not have it filled. I knew that if Melvin saw it on the back seat, he would be content. Oh, I've done this so many times – just to escape. It is better than the misery of argument.'

'And Mrs Wells?'

Vanessa smiled wanly. 'She has many good points and is very loyal.'

They walked down the steep hill from the car park, to Adrian's offices.

'Suppose,' Carla said, 'he should not be in?'

Vanessa put a hand on Carla's arm. 'Would you mind waiting with me?'

Carla knew, much to her own annoyance, that she would wait all day.

Adrian, however, was available and greeted Vanessa with warmth. He acknowledged Carla. A sense of foreboding overwhelmed

131

him. Vanessa had never come to see *him*, he had always visited Polvose.

'Is anything wrong?' he asked, as he settled them in their respective chairs. His gaze rested upon Vanessa with anxiety.

Carla felt that she was standing on an island, watching an angry tide flow by. Her heart thudded to a degree where she could have taken her pulse rate, without timing. She waited for Vanessa's answer. Would she have the courage to tell the truth?

The truth came, as Vanessa said, almost tersely, 'You know about Melvin's infidelity, but you have no idea that he intends to murder me.' She hesitated. 'I told Carla after she came to me; I was not brave enough to face it alone. Which is why I advertised as I did.'

Carla was aware of every shade of expression on Adrian's face. His eyes registered incredulity rather than anxiety.

'Could that be an exaggeration?'

'No,' came the forceful and direct reply.

Adrian said quietly, 'Infidelity need not include murder.'

Carla clenched her hands and a hammer seemed to be knocking on them. She was out of her depth, incapable of making any comment because of Adrian's hostility – carefully guarded – towards her. She waited for Vanessa's answer, every nerve and pulse throbbing.

'My death would mean nothing. Oh, I

admit that I felt I could not face it alone, but I am not going to have Carla involved.'

The silence that followed was as great as that before an earthquake. Adrian's voice changed and became as sharp as gun-fire. 'Carla involved?' Then he said gently, 'Don't worry; while Carla is with you no accidents will happen. Melvin would never be foolish enough,' he hastened, 'to involve a second person.' And even as he spoke, with all the bitterness, the surge of emotion, filled him with the hatred that was akin to love. He added deliberately, 'But would it not be better if Carla returned to Ascot? Her presence seems to be causing you anxiety.'

Only Carla understood the innuendo. Vanessa cried, 'You are not helping me: to lose Carla – if she can bear to stay – would make my life impossible and empty.'

Adrian got up from his chair and walked to a window on his right.

'And how does Carla feel about that?' He spoke as though Carla were not in the room, but Vanessa was too overwrought to notice it, as she answered, 'Carla has said she will stay… Adrian, you look so hard.'

His reply was instantaneous: 'You are here to consult me as your solicitor. I have to be objective and even brutal, but the idea that Melvin is going to murder you strikes me as fantastic.'

Vanessa listened to the words as though

they were not touching her, or registering in any way. They were the despair in her heart.

At that moment Adrian moved forward and took her hand in his. To him it was a courteous gesture; to Carla, it was evidence of his love for her. He said simply, 'Please do not worry; you will be well guarded.' This, he thought, was a matter he could discuss discreetly with the police.

Vanessa moved close to Carla and said breathlessly, 'And Carla?'

His expression changed, but only Carla was aware of it.

'Both of you will be guarded – this I promise.'

Vanessa walked a few paces away from her chair. 'Thank you,' she said weakly. 'I've been such a coward. I'm sorry.'

Adrian looked at her intently. 'I should not call myself a coward if I happened to be afraid of being murdered.'

At that moment, Carla stood in the wilderness of her own misery and loneliness. For a second, as she left the offices, she glanced over her shoulder. Adrian stood watching her. It was as although with every step she took, she was dragging his heart from his body. He knew then that he was in love with her.

Vanessa hurried back to him. 'Could you have lunch with us?' she asked, almost childishly.

Adrian hesitated, the tug of war between anger, love and the desire to be with Carla, foreign to him. All he said was, 'If you and Carla will have lunch with *me*.'

'Very well.' She smiled. 'Useless arguing with one's solicitor.'

'Useless. I'll join you at The White Hart.'

There, studying the two women as they sat over the meal, Adrian wondered if Vanessa had even a faint suspicion about Carla. Yet why should she, when everything was so discreet? Vanessa might have tuned in to some 'thought wave' of his, as she asked suddenly, 'Adrian, have you any idea who the woman in this case is? Or,' she added sadly, 'the women? It is hardly likely that there is just one.'

Carla said involuntarily, 'It has been known.' The moment she had spoken, she realised what this would convey to Adrian.

'Everything has been known.'

Vanessa rushed on, 'As I said to Carla, she could easily be in the district, or even on the estate.'

Adrian started. Did Vanessa know about the cottage? Of its existence, probably, but not the purpose it served. 'True,' he agreed.

'Time is the only factor.' Vanessa sighed in relief. 'I'm glad I have convinced you. I've sometimes thought that I was going mad. After all, that night when I was almost pushed out of the window... I knew who it was, but it would not have been so easy to prove. Where Melvin vanished to and then returned, I shall never know. Although Polvose is a labyrinth of passages, I've never tried to explore any of them. The idea of them gives me the creeps.'

'Meaning,' Adrian suggested, 'that Melvin was not on the cliff walk at the time.'

Vanessa shook her head. 'He could not have got back from there in time. I've been thinking all this out.'

'You don't like the cliff walk?' Adrian suggested.

Vanessa dug her elbows into her waist in a gesture of fear. 'I would not go along there for anything. Melvin loves it. It would be a perfect place if he could persuade me to accompany him on one of his jaunts.' She added: 'I agree with him that the view is as glorious as the path is dangerous. But it's a blind alley. Perhaps that makes him feel secure.'

Adrian spoke intently. 'I want your word that you will not go near it – ever. In any circumstances, or with anyone.'

'That's an easy enough promise to give.' Vanessa's brows puckered. 'But I don't understand the "anyone".'

'It isn't necessary for you to understand,' Adrian said firmly. 'You don't know who might come to Polvose.' His voice was authoritative. 'It isn't often that one is able to *prevent* a murder being committed – by being forewarned.'

Vanessa's eyes held both pain and relief.

'So you *believe* me.'

'I believe you,' came the swift reply.

Carla had listened in unhappy silence. Just for a fleeting second, her gaze met Adrian's, hoping for some sign, some gesture, that might bring him close.

As they left the hotel she asked herself: just where did her duty lie? Was her silence a disloyalty to Vanessa – or a protection?

8

Melvin made his way to the cottage and his anger was as dark as the clouds hanging low from the sky like tethered balloons.

Gina ran forward as his key went in the lock, her face alight with happiness. 'I hardly dared hope you'd manage today,' she cried, as her arms went around his neck, and then dropped weakly to her sides as she felt his resistance. Instantly, fear made her feel sick. Melvin stood very still, assessing her, rather than looking at her. His gaze travelled over her face, her dress.

'What is it? Darling–'

'What have you done with the brooch I

gave you?' He spoke quietly.

Gina's eyes seemed to become larger and wider. Her head moved jerkily. 'Done with it?' she echoed fearfully.

'I like to see you wearing it.'

Relief relaxed every muscle in her body and her sigh was poignant.

'Then I'll put it on,' she said swiftly, 'only I don't wear it when I'm busy around here.' As she spoke she ran to her dressing-table in the adjoining room, and took out a small trinket box, where she kept her treasures.

Melvin followed, watching her intently. As she lifted the lid, she gave a cry of dismay. 'But – but it isn't here ... yet it must be. I always keep it here.' Her gaze turned back to him in panic and appeal. Feverishly, her hands shaking, she sorted through the contents. Little whimpering noises escaped her lips. 'Perhaps it is in the drawer,' she said finally and in desperation, feeling that her heart was a lead pendulum swinging in her body. Then, 'It's gone ... oh, Melvin! Yet how? Who could have taken it?' A shudder went over her. Suppose Carla Selby–

Melvin moved closer to her and she faced him, white and stricken.

'I'd like to believe that this isn't a perfect act,' he said coldly.

Her hands went up to her face, her eyes closed. She heard his words, but they failed to register any true significance. Her

138

thoughts were scuttling madly as she tried to remember any other place in the cottage where she might accidentally have put it. Then, suddenly, she stared at him. 'Act? What do you mean?'

'Only that you left that brooch at the hotel when we stayed at Perth last. It was returned to Mrs Ingram at Polvose.' His words lashed like a whip.

The room had grown darker as the storm gathered and the sudden deathly silence was broken by Gina's horrified whisper, 'No! Oh, *no.*' She swayed and sat down on the bed. Her eyes looked up at him like those of a wounded spaniel until suddenly through the conflict and emotion, she cried, 'Why did you talk of a perfect act?'

'It could have been deliberate on your part. Not just carelessness.'

The cold sickness of hurt washed over Gina like death. 'If you can believe that of me,' she whispered brokenly, 'then you have never known me – or loved me.'

'That could be true,' he replied.

She made a little hopeless, despairing gesture. 'And what could I have hoped to gain?'

'You are the best judge of that.' His temper was rising. 'You want to *be* Mrs Ingram. Precipitating matters–'

Gina cut in, 'And do you think I should have been mad enough to endanger *us?*

Wreck our plans?'

Melvin's attitude changed. His eyes lost their wild look of suspicion. 'No,' he said, released from torment. 'No.'

They clung together, but without peace. 'Why,' he asked jerkily, 'didn't she mention that the brooch had been returned to her?' He spoke as though Gina was aware of the details and she did not make the mistake of questioning. All she said was, 'It ties up with the character which you have described to me. Oh, darling, I'll never forgive myself.'

He kissed her with a mixture of tenderness and passion. 'It won't make any difference in the end. But I've got to get hold of the letter that was sent. I don't like being in the dark over anything and how can I know if our booking was mentioned?' He was clarifying his own opinions.

'Does that fact really count? Pride could make a woman remain silent and, if she can ignore the brooch, she might just as easily tear up the letter.'

Pride, Melvin thought – and love. He might hate Vanessa, be sick to death of her, but, manlike, it touched the chord of his conceit to believe that she still cared for him. He nodded his agreement.

'My brooch,' Gina said pitifully.

Melvin's jaw tightened. 'You shall have it back,' he promised. 'And another one to go with it.' His voice was harsh with frustration, as he added, 'I shall have to cancel Perth.'

She looked up at him. 'There are many years ahead, darling.'

The words echoed thorough the stillness of the room.

'All the years – *Mrs Ingram.*'

A thought struck Carla as she and Vanessa returned to Polvose just before tea. 'Why don't you let Adrian have the brooch? Shall we say, for safe keeping.'

Vanessa responded instantly.

'Funny! I never thought of that.'

'Neither did I until now... Why did you tell Adrian of your fears? I mean – today?'

'The feeling that, since you are good enough to stay with me, you should be protected.'

Carla's expression was reflective. 'I wonder just what suddenly made Adrian believe you.'

'I've been thinking about that, and his remark about my not knowing who might come to Polvose. It gave me a creepy sensation – despite all that's happened.' Vanessa said urgently, 'Carla, will you take the brooch and the letter to Adrian this evening?'

'I?' Carla looked startled.

'Safe hands.' She added wistfully, 'Melvin will be in for dinner and I ache to talk to him. He avoids being alone with me. And I'm always scared of saying the wrong thing ... I know, yet still I go on.' Tears gushed to

Vanessa's eyes. 'We'd better get the brooch and letter now – before he comes back.'

As they went up the stairs, Mrs Wells asked if she should serve tea.

'How long has Mr Ingram been out?'

'About an hour, madam. I don't think he expected you home so early. He said he needed some air and that, when he returned, he would have some tea and sandwiches.' She hastened, 'He spoke as though he would be having the meal alone.'

Carla felt that there was something significant about those words – commonplace though they were.

'Then he will have a pleasant surprise,' Vanessa said lightly. 'We'd like tea in a few minutes.'

'And sandwiches?'

Vanessa glanced at Carla. 'Just tea for me, please.'

Mrs Wells moved noiselessly away as Vanessa said, 'And for me.'

In the bedroom Vanessa exclaimed as she went to her bureau, 'Why should Melvin speak as though he would be having the meal alone? Oh, I suppose he just hoped we might not be back.' Vanessa sighed as she clicked open the secret drawer and then gave a gasp of dismay.

'The brooch,' she cried. 'Carla, it's gone. So *that* was why Melvin wanted the house to himself.'

All the sinister forces seemed to be gathering in that room.

'Yet why should he know that it was in your possession?'

'I had a feeling he heard from the hotel this morning. It was inevitable he would do so sooner or later.'

'They could have written to *you* again.'

'Probably got cold feet in case they'd made a *faux pas*. It's just a supposition, but he was on the defensive when I mentioned his letters. Just as he always is if you touch the fringe of the truth. For once *he* will be in suspense because of my silence.'

Carla wondered how close they had come to the truth.

'When did you last open that drawer?' she asked.

Vanessa did not hesitate. 'Yesterday. I've looked at it every day. In all these years, Melvin has hardly glanced at that bureau, and I remember how bored he was when I mentioned a secret drawer.'

Carla's flesh tingled. Vanessa had given the letter into her keeping, but she had not looked at it in the meantime. Her expression conveyed a silent message, making Vanessa cry, 'Thank heaven I did not put the letter in there.'

'We'd better make sure,' Carla said breathlessly and they both hurried to the adjoining room and to the innocent-looking beauty box which contained – among the standard jars, bottles, etc. – an ordinary lipstick, into which the letter had been rolled and, at the top, a circle of cellophane placed so that a stub of the original, scooped out, lipstick could be inserted, to deceive anyone removing the outer sheath.

Vanessa gave a thankful sigh. Carla shook her head, as she noticed the angle of the stub and removing it, found the case empty. 'So much,' she said, 'for what appeared to be a perfect hiding place.' Embarrassment overwhelmed her. 'I'm so sorry,' she said, bewildered to the point of disbelief.

Vanessa's attitude was immediately consoling. 'It's not your fault. I thought the idea was brilliant... Oh, Carla, it's all so horrible. Takes away the last little feeling of security. I should have known that Melvin would never be done. If only I'd given the things to Adrian.' Her voice was flat and hopeless.

Carla glanced out of the window.

'He's just coming back,' she said breathlessly.

'Then we'd better get downstairs.'

They went quickly, reaching the hall as Melvin entered it. He started at the sight of them, a gleam of annoyance in his eyes. 'You're back,' he exclaimed sharply. 'I didn't expect you.' There was a nervous agitation in his manner that was puzzling to Carla.

'Didn't you notice the car?' Vanessa asked.

'No. You don't usually put it in the garage straight away. Are you going out again?'

'Carla is – to see Adrian.'

Carla gave Melvin stare for stare. 'I didn't put the car in the garage, but at the side entrance – in the shade.'

He gave a grunt. 'Ah, well, I've had a couple of hours in the fresh air.'

Carla and Vanessa moved into the sitting-room. Mrs Wells, thought Carla, had stated that Melvin had been out about an hour. Why the discrepancy?

Tea was brought in and Mrs Wells inquired if Melvin's headache was better.

Immediately, instinctively, Vanessa showed concern.

'The fresh air cured it,' he said in an ungracious tone. 'And don't start fussing.' He addressed Vanessa impatiently as Mrs Wells went from the room. 'I thought we were going to the cinema this evening,' he went on irrelevantly. And all the time he was studying Vanessa and seeing her through new eyes. The impact of truth difficult to accept. She sat there pouring out the tea and all the time she *knew*. His efforts to deceive her were now a farce. He visualised Gina in her place and felt a thrill of anticipation. Gina would bring Polvose to life. There would be no more conforming, no more planning and plotting – only freedom. His body heated degrees higher than his normal temperature as ideas flooded his mind. Everything was a matter of timing, he argued with himself. To give way to the hatred building up within him would achieve nothing. He found that a sense of power began to creep over him. Power that would be his ally in that second of decision. Vanessa's silence was an indictment against her. Call it love, pride – anything. It remained a weakness, nevertheless. His was the strength. His voice rapped out, 'Did you hear what I said to you?'

Vanessa flinched. 'I was waiting for you to say whether you wanted to go.'

'I can just as well be bored at the cinema as sitting about here.'

Vanessa said quietly, 'Then I wonder why you decided to remain here – instead of going away again.'

'And what is that supposed to mean?' There was fury in his dangerous calm. 'That you prefer my room to my company?'

Carla felt that the nerves in her stomach were tightly knotted.

'You know that isn't true.'

'I know nothing about you,' he retorted harshly. 'The tea wasn't sweet enough. I'll have two lumps of sugar this time.'

She took the cup from him and was shaking so violently that she spilt it in the process of reaching the slop basin. His gaze met hers in critical contempt. 'You seem upset, my dear.'

146

Carla got to her feet. She looked down at Melvin with a cold analytical distaste. 'The fresh air may have cured your head, but it certainly hasn't improved your temper – or your manners.' There was an underlying note of warning in her voice which he was quick to detect. It was a moment when his alert mind served him well. He burst into hearty laughter. 'I'll give you that one, Carla.' Charm oozed back.

Carla might not have heard him. She glanced at Vanessa and said, 'I shan't be long in Fowey.' The words echoed almost sinisterly. Vanessa's eyes seemed mutely pleading. 'Perhaps Adrian might like to come here.'

'You see,' Melvin said lightly, 'how eager my dear wife is to be alone with me.' He reached out and lifted the telephone receiver, giving Adrian's number. 'I think it an excellent idea for Adrian to come here.' In a matter of minutes the arrangements were made. He said smoothly, 'How simple everything is once a decision is made.'

And all the time words, rather like a ticker tap, were going through his brain. With Adrian there, he might have another opportunity of searching for the letter. He knew where to find the brooch…

9

Adrian felt that visiting Polvose that evening was like rubbing sandpaper into an open wound, and yet he could not resist the possibility of seeing Carla. His loves had been few, the sub-conscious desire for being loved and loving – far greater than he had ever realised. And now everything he craved was threaded into a web of deceit and bad faith. He detested the idea of having to talk to Melvin, with the mental picture of the cottage flicking through his mind like some diabolical screen-play.

As he brought his car to a standstill and entered the house, Mrs Wells hurried towards him, agitated and, to his discerning eye, overwrought. She spoke in a whisper, 'May I have a word with you, sir?'

Adrian glanced around him. No one was in sight.

'They are all in the rose garden,' she murmured. 'Waiting for you.'

Adrian met her gaze. 'I am listening, Mrs Wells.'

Mrs Wells rubbed her hands together as though she were washing them. 'You know how much Mrs Ingram means to me.

Madam' (she unconsciously reverted to the habit of years) 'has had a great shock. I know it. I can't help her, or mention it to anyone, sir.'

'Shock?' Adrian's voice dropped.

'I know. I may not know what caused it, but I just know.'

Adrian's mood was not improving, but he could not dismiss the words. 'And what do you know?' he said, as though interrogating a client. In this case he dreaded the answer.

'Miss Selby,' she said in a whisper. 'There's something very funny going on here. I knew it the day she came.'

Adrian stiffened. 'I have no intention of discussing Miss Selby with you.'

The black crow-like figure seemed to become larger and more formidable.

Adrian tried to shut down on his anger and his jealousy.

'All I care about is Madam's happiness.' She added, 'Miss Selby is not going to give it to her.'

Adrian was spared having to make a reply because Carla came into the house at that moment, entering through the French windows in the sitting-room. The sight of Adrian and Mrs Wells together (even though Mrs Wells immediately moved away) filled her with apprehension.

'I didn't realise you had arrived,' she said weakly, feeling his gaze coldly upon her. 'I was coming to see you – at Vanessa's request. But Melvin–' Confusion crept upon her at the sound of Melvin's name.

'Melvin preferred that I came here – naturally.'

Carla made no reply. She felt that she was living on a moving staircase, a puppet instead of a person; but a puppet consisting of only heartache. As they went out into the garden, where deck chairs stood under a vast cedar tree, everything around her became a mockery of desire. It was a golden evening, when river, sea and the green, sloping hills shimmered in the sun, darkness and the threat of a storm having vanished. Now and again, faintly on the breeze, came the chugging of a motor boat.

Melvin and Vanessa lay back in their respective chairs. Melvin indicated the two vacant ones. Looking at him Adrian felt homicidal. And although it was such a brief while ago that he had discovered the truth about the cottage, it seemed both a matter of minutes and a matter of years, because the disillusionment and suffering in between blanketed time. Yet he knew that he must not betray his antagonism. Melvin's voice was confident as ever. How much did Adrian know? He monopolised the conversation entirely until Wells brought out the drinks.

Listening and watching, Carla saw the

scene as a cameo of life held and projected in a distorting mirror. Anyone seeing the four of them sitting there, in that perfect setting, would automatically think in terms of the ideal. Yet there was murder, jealousy, deceit and scheming, distributed among them. Eyes met eyes, like shuttered windows, concealing every thought. Adrian despised her and, through her, Melvin, quite apart from the fearsome knowledge imparted to him that day. Vanessa was torn to the point of destruction, fighting to believe that something might save her and her marriage. And not so far away, Gina sat alone, waiting for the violence that would release her. Meanwhile what torture must she endure in the knowledge that Melvin was, at that moment, with his wife, playing the part of the respected husband. How much had he told her? And how long would she accept living in isolation? It was as if her ghost haunted Polvose.

And, suddenly, a new fear was born and Carla's protectiveness towards Vanessa increased. That brought gentleness as she looked at Adrian. If he was in love with Vanessa, his must be an almost unendurable hell. His attractiveness filled her with emotion which flowed over her body like a warm sea. He caught her gaze, and for a second it was as though moments of their earlier meetings were re-lived. She longed to be alone with him and yet dreaded the task Vanessa had asked her to undertake in telling him of the discoveries of that afternoon. Adrian was weighing up the situation and facts as he knew them and said almost abruptly, 'Do you feel like a short walk, Carla?' His laughter was false, and he added to give it a ring of truth, 'That means, of course, taking in the acres of Polvose! I don't think one could ever explore–'

Melvin's nerves snapped and he asked sharply, 'Explore. There's nothing to *explore*.'

Adrian was alive to the tension, the strain, that was threatening to make Melvin lose control. He had no wish to be instrumental in it and hastened, 'Pity! I always think it is rather like salt to an egg, to look for something unexpected round the corner.'

Melvin smiled sheepishly. He wanted to get into the house and the possibility of being thwarted infuriated him. 'Afraid I haven't that spirit.'

Adrian nodded. 'Your work really covers that.' So, he thought with unease, there *was* something *to* explore. But what? Or did the word, to Melvin, cover only the cottage? He could not believe that its existence was unknown.

Vanessa spoke almost for the first time. 'While you take Carla for a walk, I'm going inside. Too much sun makes me feel a little sick.'

'Sick?' Adrian echoed the word and Carla followed the trend of his thoughts.

Melvin said: 'Don't make it sound so dramatic! It's a common enough symptom.' He looked at Vanessa with solicitude. 'We'll go in and put on a record. You *are* pale. Music always soothes you.'

She brightened instantly. 'I'd love that. It's ages since we used the radiogram.' But even as she spoke, a pang of fear shot through her. She overcame it and smiled. Why not enjoy the moments given to her, without thinking of yesterday, or tomorrow? Melvin helped her to her feet. 'All right?'

'Yes, no fainting,' she promised.

Was this, Adrian asked, for Carla's benefit? A way of hitting back because of his jealousy? No one, he decided, could judge the motives behind that tortuous mind.

'This is one occasion,' Adrian said, when he and Carla were lost amid paved walks and flowering shrubs, 'when we shall not take the cliff walk.'

Carla kept her voice as steady as was possible. 'We shall not need to walk for more than a few minutes in any case – just long enough for me to tell you the latest development.'

He did not want to listen to her voice so that it would echo hauntingly the second he left her; yet he knew that he must hang on every word she uttered even though it meant being a traitor to the love he bore her.

'Development?' His scepticism was obvious. 'In a matter of hours?'

She told him as briefly as was possible, ending with the fact that Vanessa felt the brooch and letter had been a protection.

'And do you agree? Can there ever be any protection where there is bad faith?'

She retorted bitterly, 'No; any more than there can be justice in condemnation without a hearing.'

They had reached an isolated part of the grounds, where a series of copses dipped down to the river – the trees so green and the sea so blue that the scene might have been a painting – a masterpiece. The scent of roses hung about them, tugging sharply at the emotion lying just beneath the surface. There was something challenging as well as tantalising about Carla's imperturbability one minute and her gentle sadness the next, which confounded all his theories. For a second anger, hostility, ebbed away as they gazed in wonderment and then, turning, faced each other.

His kiss was as passionate as it was unexpected, and on his part deliberate, but his cold, clinical analysis that it was better to woo an enemy, than to be antagonistic, was lost in the tumult of increasing desire as he felt her response, and then her swift denial as she drew away from him. 'Bad faith,' she echoed scornfully.

But neither deceived the other into believing that attraction – quite apart from love – was dead.

They walked on in silence, waging a private war. Mechanically, they moved towards the spot near Carla's window. Adrian appeared indifferent, even oblivious, of the fact. Carla looked up and gave a little gasp. 'There's someone in my room.'

Adrian followed her gaze. 'How can you possibly tell that from here?'

Carla's voice was shaken. 'We're at an angle where we could see any figure, either in shadow or substance – according to their position in the room.'

'There's no sign of anyone there now.'

'I'm aware of that.'

He shot her a challenging glance, 'Would you like to prove to me that you could be either shadow or substance – by going up there now, while I wait here?'

'I'll do more than that,' she replied, 'I'll believe your verdict.'

With that she left him and went in the house by the side door, hurrying to her room. As she entered it, she had the uncanny sensation that might be felt on returning to one's house after a burglary had taken place. At first she kept back from the window and stood in the beam of sunlight which painted flickering shadows on walls and floor. Then, she swiftly walked from side to side, never pausing at the window. That done, she went swiftly downstairs, and back to where Adrian was standing.

'You were right. I could not have said it was you, unless I'd known, but there was a fleeting glance of a form in shadow.' He added, quietly, 'I'm sorry, Carla.'

She felt choked – too choked to speak.

'Let's go in,' she murmured.

Adrian dare not allow his love for her to undermine his purpose.

'Since the letter and brooch have gone, for what could anyone search?' And all the time his thoughts were racing as he recalled Mrs Wells' words.

Carla could take refuge only in attack. The memory of his kiss, the closeness and the sudden emotion, made her weak with longing.

'Nothing that I can think of. I haven't any incriminating evidence hidden away.'

He looked at her critically.

'I suggest that unless you have no objection to being one of the many women in Melvin's life, then you *must* be the one with whom he stayed in Perth... Having been entrusted with the letter, you would have been rather foolish to have kept it.'

Carla clenched her hands at her sides. 'The solicitor,' she flashed contemptuously.

The moment the words were uttered, she

was drawn back into her own net, as the memory of her remarks – the night they had dinner in Fowey – rushed back. Then she had said that she hated the solicitor, to which he had added, 'But not the man.'

Adrian was withdrawn and detached, although he recalled the incident vividly, knowing that once he joined in the recollection, his will to resist her would vanish. His voice was cold and emotionless as he retorted, 'We are necessary evils... Would you say that the figure you saw was Mrs Wells?'

'No; it was a small shadow.' She added, 'Why ask me questions when you have no intention of believing the answers?'

In the house, Melvin was saying to Vanessa, 'I hope your sickness has gone.'

'Not entirely,' Vanessa replied. She was curled up on the sofa. Suddenly the impulse to draw him close to her – an impulse born of emptiness and desolation – became compulsive. 'Melvin...' There was an unconscious note of pleading in her voice.

He stiffened. 'Well?'

'Couldn't we go away for a few days – a long week-end, perhaps?'

'Why?'

'Because it is ages since we did so.'

He thought, with self-satisfaction, that she was like clay in his hands. Yet all the time she *knew*. The fact brought with it a certain

fascination. For any woman to be so *spineless*
– even though it suited his own purpose
admirably. His nerves were taut because he
had hoped to continue his search, and yet
considered it risky until Adrian and Carla
came in.

'Hardly a stimulating reason,' he commented. He looked at her without expression
of any kind, his thoughts shut away from her,
his attitude sphinx-like. 'You are not thinking
in terms of a second honeymoon by any
chance – are you?'

Her eagerness was almost pathetic.

'That would be wonderful.'

'For you – or for me?' A faint smile
touched his lips. This was the wife hoping to
woo him away from the woman whom, no
doubt, she saw as merely a mistress.

Vanessa kept her hands clasped tightly in
her lap.

'For us both.'

'I'll think about it, darling,' he said, hearing Adrian and Carla come into the hall.
'You have an idea there. We could go up to
London.' His eyes brightened as though the
prospect pleased him. 'Ah, Adrian – Carla,
you've just interrupted a little romantic
scene. Second-honeymoon stuff and all
that. London and the noise! But who am I
to complain if that is what Vanessa wants?'

Vanessa fell into the trap he had set for
her. 'I did not say London.' Her voice was

quiet, but the remark tentative. 'You did.'

Melvin turned on his heels. 'How like a woman,' he retorted ridiculingly. 'Amazing! Never can stick to the facts. And it was she who started it all!' A sadistic gleam came into his eyes. 'I shall have to think again. Anyone who wants to go to London in June must be mad!'

Carla leapt in defensively, 'It does happen to be the season.'

'And I would like to go to the theatre, the Summer Exhibition and–'

His laughter held the indulgence one might have shown a child. 'Darling! Since when have you been interested in art?'

The room seemed to be like a vast well, filled with silence. Vanessa quivered and then said, with spirit: 'Since I was given my first paint brush. I used to paint, and was not supposed to be too bad at it.'

Carla intercepted the look that Melvin and Adrian exchanged; a look which seemed to have an element of understanding in it. She said, 'Just because you happen to possess an electronic brain, Melvin, is no reason to deprecate all the things your wife enjoys.' There was a fire in her eyes that sobered him. 'Your enjoyment in life lies in belittling everyone else.' She knew that Adrian was watching her, and she could read his thoughts as though they were on a ticker tape. To him, she was defending Vanessa, in order to keep

Melvin in her life and thus the act – as no doubt he would call it – continued.

Her summing up was correct as Adrian's keen, analytical brain assessed the value of her privilege in making such condemnatory remarks in view of her position in the house.

Melvin, scared of any eruption, laughed mirthlessly, 'Carla fulfils every obligation – even to putting me in my place!' As he spoke, his thoughts embraced only Carla's warning.

But nothing could remove Carla's feeling of dejection. Hers was an invidious position. She kept up the aggressive mood, while speaking in a manner full of innuendo. 'Can any woman put any man in his place? She merely sees through him. It could be a far greater power.'

'It could also be the same in reverse.' Adrian's voice was low yet full of meaning.

Carla forced a smile. 'The only thing men see through is cellophane.' She added, 'And not all solicitors are exempt.'

It was after Adrian had gone, and the house was taking to itself a mystery that came with night, that Vanessa went into Carla's room to spend a few minutes alone with her, while Melvin had his last drink.

'*Did* you suggest London?' Carla asked.

Vanessa seated herself in the chair by the window.

'No.' She explained the details. 'For a few

seconds I almost convinced myself that we might have a second honeymoon.'

Carla could not resist asking, 'How can you bear to sleep in the same bed with him?' The question was spoken gently and in bewilderment.

Vanessa's half smile was so sad, so pathetic, that Carla could have wept for her. 'When you live with fear, it is better to have the person you fear as close to you as possible. I'd never close my eyes if I had a room to myself, or even separate beds. Now, if he turns, or moves, I *know*.' Colour flushed her cheeks. 'He never makes love to me. That, too, is an agony. All that stopped quite a few years ago. At first, I used to rehearse long speeches about it, make up my mind to mention it. I never have. Neither has he. I expect sharing a bed is something he tolerates because he could never bear the idea of not being regarded as the happily married man. And he sleeps well.'

'His behaviour surely–'

'Ah,' Vanessa hastened, 'that's where you don't understand Melvin. He would never see, or think of, his behaviour as being other than perfect. He has no self-criticism. Everyone else is wrong – never he. I've said this before. And when he is charming one tries to forget. We all live, to some extent, in a world of hope and self-deception.' She got up quickly and hurried to the door. As she opened it, she gave a shrill cry and jumped as though she had been startled by a ghost. *'Melvin!'*

Had he been listening? Otherwise why should he have been standing so close to the door?

Immediately, he was angry. It was his only weapon.

'I've been looking everywhere for you,' he said stiffly. 'But if you care to stay up all night, do so.' He half turned and looked back over his shoulder as he added, 'By the way, instruct Mrs Wells to prepare the room on the other side of the house – the one that Carla *should* have had–' A gleam of satisfaction replaced the former anger in his eyes. 'I shall be using it in future. Oh, yes, and I want my writing desk brought up from my study – the small writing desk – and put in the window alcove. I shall sleep in the dressing-room tonight.' With that he shut the door noisily behind him.

Vanessa put both hands up to her mouth. 'I'm frightened – *frightened.*'

Carla knew that so was she.

10

Carla lay awake most of that night. Who had been in her room and why, suddenly, was Melvin leaving Vanessa's bed? Was this a dramatic gesture which he would ultimately use as a defence? It was like listening to a discordant symphony rapidly building up to a violent crescendo. She could not put Adrian out of her thoughts, any more than she could, at this stage, hope to justify herself. The weight of her responsibility towards Vanessa increased. Intuitively, she felt that her silence was vital. Melvin dare not dismiss her. Although he was not aware that she knew Gina Clements, he could never be absolutely certain as to the extent of her discoveries. And where, before he came to Polvose, his plans might be simple to execute, now they had become involved, and this was his frustration, his anger. It was terrible to watch hatred burn like a white hot fire. That hatred, she realised, had increased even during her stay in the house. Adrian's words, *'to prevent a murder'*, echoed with a degree of comfort and from it another idea sprang. Had he not promised to guard them day and night? Suppose it was he who had

sent someone to her room that night? Someone to search for any evidence that might be
incriminating? His tactics could have been
subtle and her co-operation invaluable for
his experiment. At this point, sheer exhaustion enabled her to sleep.

It was a few nights later that Adrian said to
Clark Faber, his partner, as they sat over a
night cap, 'You haven't been to Polvose
lately – why?'

'Too busy.'

'Nonsense.'

'Fine! Have it your own way!' Clark smiled
and puffed at his pipe. 'Come to think of it,
I did hear a bit of gossip' – he grinned as he
spoke – 'about the Ingrams the other night.'

'Such as?' Adrian was so alert that Clark
exclaimed, 'Good heavens, man, don't jump
out of your seat!'

'I repeat, such as?' Adrian found the
suspense unbearable.

'It was at the club–'

'It would be,' Adrian commented.

Clark sat back calmly and studied Adrian
intently. 'You're a bag of nerves, and it's
time someone took you in hand.'

'Nothing of the kind,' Adrian retorted.
'Come to the point.'

'Very well.' Clark took his pipe from his
mouth and looked at Adrian very directly.
'Some new member – can't recall his name
– mentioned Polvose. He could not find it,

and heaven knows, he has a point there. But he talked of having known the Ingrams and was at the christening of their daughter.'

Adrian tensed, but modulated his voice. 'What did you say to that?'

Clark leaned back in his chair. 'I told him that the Ingrams of Polvose had no children and that he was, obviously, looking for the wrong people.'

'Did that satisfy him?'

'It appeared to, but as the fellow and his wife were returning to London the following morning, I couldn't very well make an issue in order to prove myself right ... look here, Adrian, we've been friends, partners, for years, but I'd not retract one word I said to you some short while ago. And this time it is not something I ate for breakfast.'

'You don't have to remind me,' Adrian said flatly. '"A sinister house filled with violence."'

'Are you in love with her?' The words came quietly and with an understanding that was a shock to Adrian. Clark wasn't the *type* to think along those lines.

'With whom?'

Clark was watching every shade of expression, of emotion, on Adrian's face. 'Vanessa, of course.'

At that moment the telephone rang. Adrian reached out and put the receiver to his ear.

Vanessa's voice, muted, panic-stricken, said, 'Oh Adrian, please come. Carla's missing – I mean, she isn't in her room, or in the house.' The pause was on the note of a sob. 'I can't speak properly but–'

'I'll be with you as soon as the car will bring me.'

Clark said, as Adrian jumped up from his chair, 'You would have made a wonderful midwife.' Behind the joke lay concern.

'Thanks,' Adrian said. And added with a strange appreciation, 'I've never known you until tonight. You are not right, Clark, but that does not make you any the less discerning.' By this time, Adrian had reached the door, talking as he went.

Clark smiled. He had not really been thinking in terms of Vanessa…

When Adrian reached a point reasonably near the sign, 'POLVOSE', he stopped the car and walked the distance to the house. Everything about him was alive with the sensuousness of summer, and every nerve in his body was like that of a tooth prodded by a dentist. There was fear, anger, jealousy mixed into a terrible apprehension. To his amazement, Vanessa stood at the entrance below the window which looked down on the creek. She was distraught, almost hysterical. 'Thank God you've come. Bless you… I can't find her. I can't *find* her.' She spoke as a child might speak of a beloved nanny.

Adrian drew her into the shadows of giant elms. The moonlight touched every line on her face – its anguish, its terror, and its concern.

His first question was a result of earlier training. 'Melvin? How can you get away like this?'

Vanessa lowered her head and murmured: 'He does not sleep with me any more.' She made a sound suggestive of having cried too long. 'He never forgave me for putting Carla in the next room to ours.' Tears rolled down her cheeks. 'Or what *was* ours.' She added, 'The window in that room was for me...'

And while Adrian listened, every nerve in his body seemed to be under a drill.

'Go back to bed; lock your door and leave everything to me...' He added suddenly, 'Before you go, have you noticed anything strange tonight – any small thing?'

'Nothing,' she answered honestly.

He asked cautiously, 'Mrs Wells?' Before she could comment, he hastened, 'She would know, *sense*, if you were roaming the house.'

Vanessa shook her head. 'She is at St Blazey.'

Adrian exclaimed incredulously, 'Mrs Wells – *out?*' It was a statement, rather than a question.

'Her sister, who lives at St Blazey, is ill. Wells is in the house – in charge.'

Adrian's gaze was wandering in all directions. He asked abruptly, 'Where is Melvin's room?'

'On the other side of the house – away from the creek. It looks over the gardens.'

Adrian nodded. 'Do as I say,' he repeated, as he saw her to the front door, walking in the shadow of the trees. 'I shall be here,' he promised, 'until Carla comes back, and if anything should have happened to her–'

'Why do you say "comes back" as though you know where she might have gone?' The question hit Adrian and revealed his own weakness. He hastened, 'It wasn't that, Vannie, only Carla could easily have roamed about, searching for evidence to help you.'

'She sees through Melvin,' Vanessa said as though she had not heard his words. She caught her breath on a sob. 'I wish I did not love him.'

Adrian ignored the remark. 'Turn on your bedside lamp – you have one?'

'Yes.'

'Good. Turn it on when you are safe in your own room. I dare not come nearer than this.'

In a matter of minutes, he saw the soft glow of light from Vanessa's room. The rest of the house was in eerie darkness.

Carla was awakened from an uneasy sleep, which seemed like a nightmare. Her first thought was Vanessa. She crept out of bed and went to the window. Everything was a still as a moonlit night in the tropics – without the myriad stars. She was thankful that Mrs Wells was away and even as the thought gave her confidence, she saw Gina Clements move stealthily in the shadow of a macrocarpa hedge. Instantly, she pulled a coat from the wardrobe and flung it on as she hurried to the door. Once on the landing, she paused, her gaze on Vanessa's room. No sound came from it and she groped her way downstairs, the moonlight, penetrating the curtained windows, giving her guidance. In a matter of seconds she was out of the house, praying that she would reach Gina before she disappeared.

She succeeded. Gina's face was white and terrorised as Carla caught her arm, and half threw her into a spot which led to a sunken rose garden. 'What are you doing here?' Carla spoke in an angry whisper. Then, 'You're freezing.'

'I know; I've been here for hours.'

'Why?'

'Melvin promised to meet me... He's not ill?' The voice cracked. 'Tell me.'

'He's better in health than temper.'

The tensed body relaxed. 'I didn't realise how cold even summer nights can be, when you are standing about – just waiting.'

Carla was alert to every possibility. Had

she come here for some grim purpose? Was she to share the guilt when the time came?

'Have you been in the house?' It was a question asked tersely.

'That is my business. You won't help Vanessa by bullying me.'

'All the same, Melvin hasn't been told that I visited the cottage,' Carla rapped back, 'has he?'

'No.' Gina's attitude changed. In the moonlight her face seemed ethereal. 'Oh, please – *please* don't let him know.' She clasped her hands in supplication.

Again Carla felt the passionate sincerity flowing from a shivering girl who had waited for hours to see her lover. She said gently, 'Do you realise what you are being drawn into; what is going on in that house now?'

The answer came simply, 'If one loves enough, one does not question.'

Carla lowered her head, because there was something so sincere and so poignant, that a comment would have been an outrage. But on the heels of sentiment came reality. 'All the same, you know what he is going to do?'

Gina lifted her head and combed her icy fingers through her hair. 'You would not expect me to answer that question. All I know is that whatever he does, I shall be there – beside him.' Her eyes burned with a fervour that Carla had never seen before. 'One day you will love enough to understand what I mean…' Her eyes were focusing on a spot near the house. 'He's coming … go – *please* go.' She added, 'And don't let anyone see you.'

'You are in no position to give me orders.'

'True.' It was a whisper. 'But you are not the kind of person to hurt. Death is far kinder than hurt. One is of the body, the other, the mind.'

Carla, amazed at herself, crept away. She tried to visualise herself in Gina's place and found it impossible, because there was no violence in her. At that point her thoughts petrified, and then flowed out again like a river halted by a dam. If Adrian loved her how could she say to what lengths she would go? Every day, week, or month, a woman who had been half murdered pleaded for the man she loved. She would excuse him because he was never just a husband, a lover. He was half child, who could always be cradled in her arms – no matter how great the passion that surged. At that moment she longed for Adrian as she could never have dreamed of longing for any man. She wanted the comfort of his arms around her and although she hated the sentiment, a shoulder to cry on. She stumbled back to the house, always keeping in shadow. And when she reached the door, Adrian stepped forward.

11

Carla saw the anger on Adrian's face, and shrank from it. 'Do you want to wreck Vanessa's life completely – or what is left of it?' His voice was cold and curt.

Alarm at his presence gave her the courage to ask fearfully, 'What are you doing here?'

He told her, ending with, 'Now that Melvin is sleeping on the other side of the house, your meetings will be simpler – not always at the cottage.'

Carla's nerves were frayed as it was, but the injustice infuriated her. 'I had my reasons for coming out here tonight, and they were in Vanessa's interest. I saw someone moving about in the grounds.' She added cynically, 'Your day and night guard must be very elusive – that is, if he exists.'

'He exists.' Their eyes met. Carla tried to keep her voice steady as she commented, 'It must be wonderful to have such complete confidence in oneself...' She shivered and immediately he betrayed his concern. 'Go in.' He made the words sound like an order.

'I think I'll wait for Melvin.'

'Ah! So he is out of the house. I hardly thought you would be alone, although his room would, surely, have been more comfortable.'

'You are not only insulting, you are a fool.' And with that she went into the house and shut the door.

Vanessa cried, 'Thank God, you're back. I've been crazy with worry. Did you see Adrian?'

'Yes.'

'I've made some tea,' Vanessa said disjointedly. 'You'll have to pour it out, I'm trembling too much.' She looked at Carla, adding, 'I was afraid something had happened to you ... or that you'd just gone. It made me realise, more than ever, what you mean to me and how much you do for me.'

Carla said quietly, 'I should never "just go"!... That I promise.'

Melvin's voice boomed through the hall.

'What is all this?' he demanded, irritably. He had seen the lights go on in the house and hurried back. Then, 'Good God, Adrian!' As Adrian came in, Melvin looked from face to face. 'Well! Have you been struck dumb, woman? He addressed Vanessa who explained what had happened. Her voice was full of fear, because she knew what his reactions would be.

'Of all the damn fool things to do,' he said, his temper rising. 'Dragging Adrian up here... What was wrong with wakening me?'

Vanessa was staring at him intently. 'Would

you have been in your room?'

Melvin tightened the cord of his dressing gown and blustered, 'Where else? I don't go roaming around the place at night like Carla.'

Adrian's gaze took in the fact that Melvin had a jacket on under his dressing gown.

Vanessa found the courage to say, 'All the same you have been out, or you would not have put on your shoes, instead of your bedroom slippers. And your shoes are wet.'

Carla felt a tremor of fear as she watched Melvin's face pale and his lips tighten before he shouted, 'Perhaps you followed me. This is my house and my land and I shall go where I please and do what I please. Is that understood? And any more remarks like that from you–' He thumped the table as he spoke. 'But since you must know, I saw someone lurking in the garden. Satisfied?' With that he stalked from the room in a fury. He returned almost immediately. 'And I can tell you something else … Mrs Wells hasn't gone to any sister. She was out there by the greenhouse.' A self-satisfied expression smoothed away the anger. 'She did not see me.'

Vanessa gave a little gasp as Melvin went out and slammed the door.

Adrian experienced a sensation of disquiet. Since Mrs Wells lived in the house, what purpose could she have for pretending to leave it, in order to roam the grounds? There could be only one answer. Carla. She was, to her, the enemy. But would she be capable of violence? He looked at Carla, now sitting, legs tucked under her, in an armchair which made her seem smaller and slimmer than ever. Her royal blue coat covered a flimsy nightdress, the frill of which was visible. She was pale and taut and he could not endure the idea of her being mixed up in this tragic, but sordid, situation. Perhaps Melvin, on his own with her, was an entirely different man. Perhaps the scenes with Vanessa were for her benefit. They must, he argued, have some very water-tight plan for the future. Once again he reminded himself that to relax vigilance in order to try to exonerate her would be the madness of love, without the sanity of reason.

Carla said swiftly, 'Melvin could have said that for dramatic effect!'

Adrian eyed her with merciless directness. 'I cannot think of any less likely explanation.'

Vanessa stared at them, seeming faraway. 'I've never found Mrs Wells out in any lie,' she said quietly. 'And she has a sister who lives in St Blazey.'

Adrian nodded. 'Look here, you both go back to bed. Leave this to me.'

Vanessa whispered, 'I don't want to go upstairs. I'm afraid.'

'I'll see you both up,' Adrian said.

They went and when they reached the door of Vanessa's room, he said, 'Lock your door.' He followed Vanessa's gaze. The door stood ajar.

'The key,' she said terrorised, 'has gone.' She clung to Adrian's arm and the house seemed to shudder with her.

'Has Carla's room this type of key?' he asked.

'Yes,' Vanessa whispered.

The house, although almost empty, seemed alive with the mystery surrounding ghosts. 'And does Melvin know you have locked your door since he ceased to occupy this room?'

'Yes,' she said again, dejected now, more than afraid. 'He tried it last night.'

'You are certain it was he?'

Vanessa's eyes widened. 'Who else?'

'But he did not speak?'

'No. I'd been in bed some time; the light was out, but the moon was so bright I could see everything, and I saw the door handle turn without sound and then go back again. I didn't move, or make a sound. I felt safe because it *was* locked. I even tried to tell myself that I had dreamed it. Only I know I had done nothing of the kind.'

Carla cried, 'But why didn't you say anything?'

Vanessa sat down on the edge of the bed.

'I'm rather tired of saying things. Sometimes I wonder if I am quite sane. And I'm awfully sorry, but I'm going to faint.'

Later, recovered, she said with a sudden gasp of understanding, 'Melvin thinks that if I can be frightened enough *Carla will change rooms with me.*' Her sign was half a sob. 'Then he will have me where he wants me – back at that window.'

There was a thread of logic in the deduction. 'But you *could* lock that door.'

She agreed. 'But I know – I feel it – that there is some other way *into* that room, quite apart from the door. I've said so before.'

Adrian looked at Carla and could not deaden love sufficiently to overcome fear for her, yet immediately on its heels, the idea struck him like a blow. That being the case, with Melvin sleeping in another room, he could always have access to Carla's. A convenient method.

The thought uppermost in his mind was deadly and insidious: Melvin's plan for murder might well be to drive Vanessa to suicide. Her nerves were as taut as a violin string and she was, obviously, far from being physically well. To live under strain and mental anguish, together with terror, would break even the strongest will. He said, trying to keep the bitterness from his voice, 'Perhaps Carla might do some more exploring. In any case, I shall.' He looked at Vanessa with a gentle sympathy and sadness. 'It is time you rested. Perhaps you could sleep in another room tonight.'

'No.' The answer held a note of faint hysteria. 'This was our room. I'll not leave it, and Melvin, strange though it seems, would be furious if I did. He is not the fit man you believe him to be. His rages–' She stopped. 'Never mind.'

Adrian and Carla left her at her own request. She was all right, she promised, and *was* tired. Carla followed Adrian down the stairs, catching up with him as he reached the hall. The grandfather clock struck one and the sound was like music that had come down through the years. They looked at each other, taut, anxious.

'Do you think Mrs Wells is out of the house?'

It was the last question he had expected to be asked.

'What is it you are afraid of about her? That she knows too much about you?'

Carla stood so still for a second that she might have been in a trance, then, 'Good night, Adrian,' she said quietly, and went back up stairs. The front door shut and fear lurked in every shadow. She dreaded reaching the landing which seemed always to chill her spine and prod at every nerve, as though it was concealing some dark secret which she was destined to discover. At the turn of the stairs, she realised she had not locked, or bolted, the front door and went back to do so, not looking to right, or left. Her legs felt useless as fright paralysed them. Had Adrian gone? She opened the door a matter of inches, letting out a ribbon of light and saw his tall figure and the glow of a newly lit cigarette. His ears and eyes were attuned to every sound and gesture, and instantly he moved the few steps to the house.

'Carla.'

'I forgot to lock the door.'

Relief overwhelmed him. Her eyes were dark and haunting in a face which moonlight made paler. They stood there, she clutching the door, he uncertain. There were no words to be said, but the silence was that of great emptiness. It was a second when their relationship trembled on the brink of explanation and understanding. Carla knew she was going to cry. She nodded mutely, shut the door, locked and bolted it. Sobs racked her and she fed them on anger – the anger of hurt and emotion denied. Then, once more, she faced the ordeal of getting to her own room. The staircase appeared to have lengthened, the shadows to have become grotesque ... three more stairs before she reached the turn which enabled her to look up at the landing. That was better, now she could see.

And suddenly she felt, rather than heard, footsteps and a presence behind her and stood, not daring to move. She knew who it was and that made it worse, because no one in her life had filled her with such blind terror, or revulsion, before. She did not speak, but went on until she could grasp the top of the landing rails. Then she looked down into those piercing eyes and mustered every scrap of courage as she said: 'I hope your sister is better, Mrs Wells. As you were seen in the grounds, some while ago, I assumed you had not been to St Blazey, or ever had any intention of going. Goodnight.' With that, she went into her room, seething, aware that she had increased the enmity, but finding in those few words a release from her own tensions, miseries and fears.

She crept into bed and, within seconds, fell asleep from exhaustion.

A knock on her door after what might have been, for her, minutes, or hours, awakened her. 'Who is it?' Her voice was sharp; a voice from which the drowsiness of sleep had gone. She switched on the light and saw Mrs Wells framed in the doorway. 'You.'

'I must speak to you.'

The closing of the door sounded like a trap shutting.

'We've nothing to say to each other.'

Mrs Wells moved and stood respectfully at the bottom of the bed. No one could pierce her reserve. And no one would ever fathom the working of her mind.

'I stayed here because of Mrs Ingram – because of Madam.'

'You mean she asked you to do so?' Carla was instantly alert.

'No, but because funny things are going on in this house.' Mrs Wells watched Carla with a shrewd, calculating gaze.

'That could mean anything, Mrs Wells.'

'There has been someone creeping about this house lately, and it isn't anyone who lives in it. I am afraid for Madam.' She inclined her head in deference.

Carla hoped that she did not betray the alarm she felt – without quite succeeding. She tried to modulate her voice as she repeated the words that had been uttered. Then, with swiftness, she added, 'And could you recognise the person?'

'I think so.'

Carla became challenging. 'Mrs Wells, I have been here long enough to know a little about you. You are observant and always aware of events taking place around you. I'll repeat my question, because I cannot accept your answer. It is now four o'clock in the morning and–'

'I wanted to talk to you when you *came in*.' Mrs Wells wanted to draw fire, to discover, in her own fashion, just what had happened *in* the house that night.

Carla ignored that, sensing its danger.

Mrs Wells, quick to realise that she had failed on that count, said, 'I have not seen her face.'

'Her?'

'Yes. Once, earlier this evening, I saw her feet.' She added, with a little understandable triumph in the circumstances, 'They were hurrying into *your* room.'

Carla's first thought was: Gina. So it was Gina. 'Is that all you have ever seen of her?'

'No, I caught sight of her as she ran from the house. She wore a scarf. That I remember very clearly. And a short coat. I could not rightly say what colour. It blended in with everything – like camouflage during the war – but you are too young to know anything of that.'

Carla was not deceived, but she said, 'I have read a little and seen a little about both wars, Mrs Wells. What I would like to know is why come to me about all this?'

It was not the reaction counted on.

'I – I thought you would help me.'

Carla was calm now, and she gave stare for stare. 'I think I can. When next you see someone creeping about the house, raise the alarm, so that the intruder can be caught.'

Mrs Wells said archly, 'Of course if you do not mind someone searching your room–'

'I mind your silence – having seen someone enter it. This is a matter for Mr Ingram to deal with.' As she spoke, Carla put out her hand towards the bedside lamp.

The stumpy figure turned. 'When the trouble comes, don't expect any support from me.'

'That is the last thing I should ever expect.' She switched off the light as Mrs Wells reached the door.

'Or from Mr Grant.'

Silence came again. Carla crept out of bed and went to the window. The moon was paling in a sky quivering on the brink of a dawn about to transform the beauty of the scene around her and touch it with the magic of colour speared through the sky. The thought in her mind was Gina. Had she been delegated the grisly task? Or was she searching for the letter? Carla started to shiver and locked her door. Was Vanessa right about another method of entry into the room? The one possibility had, as she was told, been sealed up. But how well? Carla disliked building up facts from fiction and while she went carefully from wall to wall, alert and prepared for some panel to shoot open at a touch, intuitively she knew she would not find one. Whatever secrets the room held would not be revealed to her, or to anyone else, at that stage.

It was about a week later that Vanessa swirled into Carla's bedroom and said, her eyes bright and sparkling, 'We're going to have that holiday! We're going away for a month.' Colour mounted her cheeks, as she added, 'He came back to me last night – really back... Oh, Carla, I'm so *happy*.'

Carla's smile was deceptive. 'This is wonderful.'

'He told me about Perth, and how he had cancelled that other booking.' A shyness came over her, as she added, 'I suppose I must have lived with hurt so long that I just could not believe he loved me.' She looked almost apologetic. 'This must seem so strange to you.'

Carla felt a pang of fear greater than anything she had known before. 'Nothing is strange to me, or crazy, where love is concerned – except love itself!'

Vanessa was living in a word of her own at that moment. 'And he said how sorry he was. He has never apologised in his life before.'

Carla could not say, 'And you believe him?' Or that 'The leopard never changes its spots.' In that moment, she saw the simple, naïve quality which had enabled Vanessa to support a man of Melvin's calibre. He must have realised that his outbursts of temper had made his position at Polvose suspect – to say nothing of Gina's presence. Out of the country, it would be another matter. She could imagine his assessing his return to a double bed as being more important since he had previously left it. Or had he quarrelled with Gina? Man-like, returning to his armchair – the sexual aspect following inevitably. Honesty and concern forced the words from her, 'And you are no longer afraid?'

Vanessa gave a sigh that was half happiness and half resignation. 'I am no longer afraid of being afraid. My life in exchange for being loved again – even for a month – would be worth it.' There was nothing dramatic in the tone of her voice, or her attitude. 'I did not ask him any questions,' she added suddenly, 'when one has been so miserable, almost suicidal' (long afterwards Carla remembered those words), 'one does not tear ecstasy apart.' There was an unconscious poignancy in the way she spoke. 'I will admit that there have been many times in my life when I think that if any man had given me tenderness, or made love to me, I could have been unfaithful. I never have.'

Carla saw Melvin that evening (Vanessa and she having been out most of the day, buying clothes), and he sensed her suspicion as she said, 'So you are taking Vanessa on holiday…' Her pause held significance.

'You make it sound like an accusation.' And although his words were firm, he moved awkwardly from one foot to the other, swiftly changing the subject. 'You will return to Ascot, I take it.'

'Meaning you do not wish me to come back here?'

'Nothing of the kind. That is the last thing.'

She stared him out. 'In any case I shall stay at Polvose until Vanessa wishes me to go.'

To her amazement, he said quietly, 'I respect you for that. In fact, I respect you in every way. You have been a great help.'

Carla studied him as though he were the first Henry Moore statue. He was so abstract at that moment that his face might have been just a hole, representing life. She dared not speak of Gina, because she felt it would be a wrong move. The atmosphere was tense and his awkwardness made her feel – quite unaccountably – a pang of sorrow for his weaknesses. It was simple to live with strength; difficult to live with weakness. She said quietly, 'Then *you* be a help, also.'

He looked at her rather like a blind man trying to regain his sight. 'I do not,' he said, with sudden passion, 'want to be a help. All I ask is to be a human being.'

Carla, feeling that Vanessa was safe for a short while, went to see Adrian that evening. He received her with amazement, but when she had told him the facts about the holiday his attitude changed immediately.

'I see your point,' he said, with a trace of bitterness. 'No woman would wish her lover to take his wife away for a month.' The words came with all the coolness of iced water – and it might have been thrown in her face.

'I was thinking of her safety...'

Clark Faber entered the room at that moment, and after he had been introduced to Carla, said, 'You are finding things difficult, Miss Selby.'

'Very.' Her gaze was direct.

Clark took out his tobacco pouch and began to fill his pipe with the care and precision common to pipe smokers. Even the way he held the match, and looked at her above its flame, was contemplative.

'I would get back to your parents as quickly as possible.'

Adrian protested irrationally, 'Carla took a job at Polvose and–'

Clark smiled. 'We have all taken jobs, started careers, and at any level, they are unknown quantities.' And all the time he spoke he was overtly watching Adrian. No question about it, Adrian was in love, jealous, and difficult. The three things made discussion almost impossible.

Carla warmed to this easygoing man who she felt would understand a great deal for which he was not given credit. She said, 'I haven't the temperament to back out without being proved either right, or wrong. I like conclusions drawn, and the opportunity given to me to apologise.' She accepted the sherry Clark gave her, adding, 'It was foolish of me to bother Adrian with the problem.'

Adrian looked annoyed. 'I am not bothered by it. I am merely summing the situation up.'

Clark pressed the tobacco deeper into his pipe and looked up from the task. 'If you ask me, Adrian, you are in a state of mind where you cannot see the wood for the trees... Sorry, Miss Selby, I have a committee meeting at the Golf Club. I hope we meet again.'

'So do I,' Carla said genuinely.

Alone with Adrian, she looked at him, picked up her bag and gloves, and moved towards the door.

'Goodbye,' she said politely.

He barred the way out of the room.

'May I be permitted to sum the situation up?'

Fairness made her say, 'Yes.'

He refused to allow her gaze to wander from his. 'People in love can behave more like idiots than sane people. You and Melvin must realise that you cannot go on in this fashion. This is just a subtle move.'

'But not for the reason you assume.' Her gaze was critical. 'You are not very good when it comes to investigation. I would not like you to brief counsel for me had I committed a crime.'

'You cannot stay at Polvose on your own.' The words were so irrelevant that, for a moment, she was lost.

'Thank you for being concerned about me. I find it touching.'

He wanted to put his arms round her, make love to her. No desire in his life had ever been so great. His anger and frustration fed on memory.

Carla felt his misery. His love for Vanessa could not fail to breed a jealousy and hurt. But as she looked at him, all the warmth and gentleness of which she was capable cancelled out every other emotion. She could not tell him that unless she was dismissed from Polvose, she would remain there because she was not strong enough to say goodbye to *him* – no matter how much she despised herself for the weakness.

'You are determined to misunderstand me.'

'On the contrary.' Her expression was, to him, baffling. 'I wonder just how long I shall be at Polvose alone.'

'Meaning?' He was instantly alert.

'You are the solicitor; you have all the clues.' A faint smile touched her lips. 'I must say that, to me, you do not appear to have any.'

Adrian responded. 'And I would say you are ahead of them all.' As he spoke, he opened the door for her, asking himself how

189

it was possible to love and hate a woman at the same time. She had the ability to make him uncertain even of his facts, and to smash his preconceived ideas.

They had reached the front door and the evening light suddenly poured over them in a rainbow of colour from the setting sun. It was a night when happiness, and all that went with it, could take wings; yet all they both felt was the hunger and longing.

'I'm afraid,' he said unexpectedly, 'that I have not been of help to you.'

She looked up at him. 'I shall not worry you again, Adrian.'

12

Carla returned to Polvose to find Vanessa busy sorting out her clothes. 'Melvin liked all the things we bought today,' she said brightly. She met Carla's puzzled gaze. Instantly, her mood changed. 'Is something wrong?' She moved swiftly to Carla's side.

The last thing Carla wanted to do was to create uneasiness in Vanessa's mind. But she had to know one thing in order to protect her.

'When Melvin told you about Perth, did he mention the name of the woman?'

190

'I didn't ask him. What he said was that it had been an infatuation which was now over – just one of those things.' Anxiety clouded her eyes. 'Why do you ask?'

Carla hastened, 'I was just wondering about the brooch and the letter.'

'He hasn't either. We misjudged him. He thinks Mrs Wells might have them. I do not mind now.' Vanessa gave a little laugh. 'I've had my hell over all that, and I don't want to dwell on it, or know the woman's name. She is not *Mrs Ingram*. I am. Why ruin today and tomorrow? I don't deceive myself, Carla. Had I started questioning him – after he had been honest with me – there would not have been any hope for us in the future.' She added wisely, 'A woman is flattered by being asked questions; a man feels it an intrusion which he resents.' A shadow crept over her face. 'Perhaps the tragedy is that the man who can crucify one can, equally, give the greatest happiness.' She went on solemnly, 'I must make you believe that I am prepared for whatever happens while we are away.'

Carla could not resist the words, 'And you love him enough for that?'

Vanessa sighed. 'Marriage makes love expendable – there is no question of *enough*. When you marry you will remember my words.'

Carla could not bear the quiet acceptance in Vanessa's voice and she cried, 'I do not want to *remember* your words, I want to hear them!'

Vanessa put a new coat in the wardrobe and looked over her shoulder as she did so. 'Never forget that this is the only happiness for me.'

Carla said bleakly, 'When do you want me to go?'

'*Go?* Never, if I could be selfish. My greatest joy would be for you to welcome us home.'

Carla wanted to cry. She knew that behind the gaiety, the restoration of a normal husband and wife relationship, the fear remained. Vanessa was putting on an act – not where her love for Melvin was concerned, but an act designed to protect him. 'If that is what you want, then I shall be here.'

The room suddenly had a stillness which Carla never forgot. It was as though the world had died around them, and they were standing in the ruins of yesterday.

Vanessa's voice changed; her expression became anxious. 'Carla, have *you* seen anyone – any stranger – in this house?'

Carla said deliberately, 'You mean a ghost?' She endeavoured to sound incredulous.

'No. It was dark and I was frightened. Afterwards, I told myself that I'd been imagining things. Although that seemed most likely, some instinct tells me that I was right.'

Carla hastened, 'Probably Mrs Wells. She

192

has the amazing habit of wandering around.'

Vanessa shook her head. 'I should have smelt the moth balls – she always has that funny smell about her.'

Carla agreed, with a nod. 'I think you have been so tense, that any shadow could be a person. Imagination can run riot, you know.'

'Not when it comes to the key disappearing,' Vanessa said quietly. 'I haven't *forgotten* anything because of Melvin's attitude.'

'It could be associated with Adrian. People delegated to guard you cannot always be invisible.' And all the time Carla was thinking of the brooch and the letter. Why should Melvin involve Mrs Wells? Mrs Wells was the last person to remove evidence of any kind which might benefit Vanessa. Everything suddenly held a new terror. There was something doubly uncanny about this holiday, and it seemed that Vanessa's bravery in contemplating it held a terrible inevitability.

That night Carla nerved herself to make her way to the cottage. It lay in shadow, desolate, deserted. The crackling of a few dried twigs beneath her feet, betrayed her presence and immediately Gina came out, a candle held in her shaking hand.

'Darling…'

Carla's face was revealed in the flickering flame.

'You!' There was the despair of disappointment in her voice.

'I want to talk to you,' Carla said firmly.

'Very well.' Resignation echoed in the words.

They moved inside and the single candle in the gloom added to the drama.

Carla went straight to the point. 'You've been haunting Polvose recently. You've been seen not only by me, but by the housekeeper and Mrs Ingram. Unless this stops, I shall tell the truth about you. It is as simple as that.'

'You still would not hurt her.'

Carla was aware, even in the dim light, of the hunted look in Gina's eyes and that her voice had lost confidence.

'It would be the lesser evil.'

At that Gina gave a little gasp which trailed away into desperation.

'No,' she cried. 'No.'

The candle flickered and spluttered, the wax running down the Chianti bottle in which it was held.

'Why do you come there?'

'At first because I wanted to find the brooch and the letter.' She added wretchedly, 'You see, it was my fault in the beginning. I wanted my brooch back. He promised I should have it.' Her voice broke. 'I didn't want the evidence to spoil everything, either.'

Carla weighed up her own words carefully. 'The hotel register would be the evidence.'

'I know that, but I know, also, that whoever has my brooch and the letter must have some good reason for keeping quiet.'

Carla asked tersely, 'Was that why you searched my room, too?' She added scornfully, 'I don't go in for blackmail.'

Gina sat up in her chair. 'Why do you use that word?'

'Wasn't it in your mind?'

'Yes.' The truth came out, and Carla realised that she herself had not taken the possibility into account. She had been so obsessed by Vanessa holding some trump card for her own protection, that she had lost sight of everything else. Gina rushed on. 'Not in the money sense, but as a weapon against me. To try to force me out of his life and ruin everything.' She added hopelessly, 'You don't understand and I can't tell you.'

'I have a good memory and recall everything you said to me on that first visit.' Carla wondered if this girl knew about the trip to Paris, and whether mentioning it would add to Vanessa's danger. She decided that silence was the best policy.

Gina nodded. Then she burst out, 'I get worried when I can't see him – cut off. And he was angry that night when you found me in the garden. I never used to be frightened. Now, sometimes, I am. Worry makes everything distorted.'

Carla tried to ask a question without appearing to do so. 'And can't you see him?'

'Not nearly so often ... why should I tell you?' Anger flashed into her eyes and then vanished. 'But you have kept quiet about me–'

Carla interrupted sternly, 'If you ever come to Polvose again, I shall call the police without saying a word to Melvin. I should not risk that, if I were you – you are hardly in any position to defend yourself.'

Gina replied with a touch of defiance, 'I shall never come to Polvose again *unless it is through the front door.* I know you mean what you say. So do I.' She stopped, instantly alert, then whispered, 'What was that – that noise?'

Carla felt that an icy wind was blowing over her.

'Don't move,' Gina said in a breath. 'We cannot be seen because the curtains are heavy and no light gets in, or out, when they are drawn, but the floor boards creak.'

They sat in an agony of suspense, hearing muted sounds, the faint breaking of twigs and an uncanny shuffling noise. Then, suddenly, all was quiet – the quietness of a graveyard.

Gina said fearfully, 'You're the only person ever to have come here...'

'But you must realise that this cottage is known to people.'

'I did not want to think of that.'

Carla thought of the journey back alone

and shrank from the ordeal. Her mouth was dry. The terror of the unknown touched her as though it had taken the shape of a dead hand. 'It was probably a rabbit or bird – one imagines hearing weird sounds at night.' Her gaze rested on Gina's white face. To be there alone in her particular circumstances called for supreme courage – no matter how unworthy the cause.

The words did not deceive either of them. Carla got to her feet.

'I'll look out,' Gina said, 'and make sure it is all right. I know every nook … I could walk blindfolded.'

Carla had the uncanny sensation that unseen eyes were watching – eyes capable of penetrating even the heavy dark curtains.

'There's no one,' Gina said thankfully, as she returned to the room. 'Go now – quickly.'

They looked at each other, drawn almost by their differences to a point of under-standing.

'I'll see you through the tunnel,' Gina exclaimed unexpectedly, when they reached the front door. 'If there should be anyone, I can disappear far quicker–' She stopped, her eyes wide. 'You're afraid of me,' she cried. 'I saw your expression.' Her voice hardened. 'I should have thought your intelligence would have made you realise–'

Carla cut in with, 'I'm sorry.'

'That's all right.' It was a cynical sound. 'You have a torch. Keep the light down.' With that she closed the door.

The atmosphere at Polvose changed miraculously as preparations for the holiday progressed. To Carla it took the form of a grotesque charade. Vanessa reminded her of a dancing doll – overwound. Melvin hid the almost satanic gleam – which flashed now and then into his eyes – behind a smile which was as deceptive as it appeared charming. It was impossible to penetrate the wall of his defence and he would retreat behind it in a silence which Carla found deadly, thankful that Vanessa seemed oblivious of it.

For all that, he said gaily one morning – three days before they were due to fly to Paris– 'We must have the Fairbrights, Malcolm and Joan and Adrian and Clark in for drinks before we leave. Heavens, we haven't seen Malcolm and Joan for ages.'

Vanessa stared at him.

'What,' he half demanded, 'are you looking at me like that for?'

'Only that Joan was killed in a car crash just before Carla came here.'

Melvin muttered, 'Good God, so she was... Car crash... Terrible of me to have forgotten. I remember now. Trouble is we see so few people here. Perhaps it isn't good for us.'

Carla sat, feeling rigid. Where was the link up between that loss of memory and his own intentions?

'Anyway,' he went on, 'sad though it is, we can still have our drinks with the others... Pity your parents aren't down here, Carla. When we get back, you must persuade them to come to stay.'

Carla thanked him. Mrs Wells, bringing in fresh coffee, flashed her a look of such enmity that Melvin noticed it. Instantly, his temper flared. 'And perhaps you could smile, Mrs Wells – just to make a pleasant change.'

She ignored the remark, set the coffee pot on the sideboard and went silently out of the room.

'They may be good servants,' he muttered, 'but they're a pain in the neck to me... Yes, more coffee, darling... We could have dinner as well as cocktails. You and Carla arrange it. I'm going into St Austell this morning to the bank to collect the travellers' cheques, etc.' He glanced at his watch. Then, 'Paris,' he said reminiscently. 'The perfect place for a second honeymoon.' He added swiftly, 'Or a first.'

Carla was watching Vanessa's face, expecting to see her smile. Instead she saw her wince.

When Melvin had gone Vanessa, now arranging flowers, said, 'I've not told you,

199

Carla. Melvin had been married before. His wife died after only three years.' She added gently, 'I'd hate you to discover this while we are away. It was only when Melvin forgot Joan's death, that I realised ... I can't quite explain.'

Carla made a helpless gesture. 'Then why *Paris*, now?'

'Because it will please him, and I don't mind – honestly.' She hesitated and the juxtaposition of ideas seemed very strange, as she went on, 'About the bank...'

'Bank?' Carla echoed the word incredulously.

'Yes, I know it sounds odd to mention it just now, but you see, Melvin has his account at Head Office in London, and a drawing account in Fowey – not St Austell. I have my account at Fowey. I've never heard him speak of St Austell, in the bank account sense. On the other hand, he is so secretive – even over the most trivial things.'

Carla had not missed either of the facts. Had St Austell anything to do with Gina?

At that moment Gina was in Melvin's arms. Few words were spoken when he reached the cottage and none seemed necessary. It was only as they sat, finally, having a cocktail, that Melvin said, 'Darling, I want you to listen to me very carefully, and not question what I ask you to do.'

Gina's nerves and stomach felt that they

200

were part of a bumpy lift. She nodded.

'I am going away for a month and during that time, I want you to leave here.'

The pain in her eyes made him hasten, 'For our good.'

'Oh!' She lowered her head for a second before asking weakly, 'Where do you want me to go?'

'London, where I can always find you,' he said promptly.

Again she nodded, but an icy hand touched her heart. 'Do you have to go away?' Her voice broke.

'Because of you – yes.' His voice was curt.

'Me?'

'Do you imagine I am so stupid that I do not hear the gossip in my own house and in the district?'

'But–'

'You've been prowling around, and this is the only way to avoid complications. You overlooked the moving black tombstone in the form of Mrs Wells. She could – and would – destroy us.'

Gina told herself that whatever happened she must not cry, but sobs were choking her, the deep aching misery of years, the isolation, the loneliness, seeming to rise like a mountain barring her way to any light.

'Are you listening?' Melvin said, with slight impatience.

'To every word,' she whispered.

'Don't forget, also, that your stupidity, in the first place, started all this.' He added gently, 'Darling, we don't want to go back over it. All I care about is ensuring our future.'

'Truly?' It came as an appeal.

'Truly.' He got up and put his arms around her. 'I know what I'm doing, but I cannot discuss it – either for your sake, or mine. I want you out of this.'

Gina put the weight of her body against his, her arms around his neck. 'Just tell me,' she said.

He took a sealed envelope from his pocket. 'Open this when I've gone. There is no message inside it, but there is more than enough to take care of you, until I am back to do so. Take a flat in London – the centre – and write c/o my bank in London. The address you already know. That way, we can be in touch. But not immediately.'

'What is "immediately"?' she asked.

'Three weeks. A formal letter,' he added swiftly. 'Then I shall be able to come to you on my return...'

She looked around helplessly. 'What about everything here? I can't leave it like this.'

'Why not? We can take care of it all afterwards. This is my land – *my land*,' he said. 'No one has ever dared to trespass and they would not know how, in any case.'

Gina could not rid herself of a certain

guilt because she had not mentioned Carla, but she knew that to do so now would complicate things, and serve no good purpose. Carla would have no reason to bother with her provided their bargain was kept.

'And suppose anyone should arrive at this cottage – it is *still mine*.' He was aggressive. 'Just as the cove is mine – everything.' He made a sweeping gesture. 'And you know the way into Fowey without attracting attention – if anyone does! You can go up to London by train from Par and book in at any hotel you choose.'

'And if I should not be able to find a flat in the time?'

'You can remain at the hotel. I shall come there.' He smiled. 'You'll get a service flat easily enough. Try one of the Court blocks.' He looked anxiously at his watch. 'I must get back. I've been here two hours.' His gaze rested on her face with what seemed a lingering tenderness. 'I don't have to tell you not to speak to anyone on the train.'

'Or off it,' she promised.

'You will have to give an address when you book in at the hotel. Think one out. And be Miss.'

'And references for any flat?'

'On second thoughts, better stay at the hotel. Paying your bill is the only passport you need then.'

'I shall give an address north of London. Be the provincial.'

'Good idea.' He glanced at the envelope. 'Guard that with your life.' He sighed. 'And remember I love you.'

She clung to him, the terror of presentiment overwhelming her. 'Darling...'

He had moved away, and the look he gave her was almost warning. He did not want to be questioned. 'What is it?'

'Nothing,' she said weakly, while knowing that there was something about all this that did not ring true.

'Enjoy London,' he said with amazing calm, adding swiftly, 'until we can do so together.'

When he had gone she sat staring into space not daring to allow her thoughts to take fearsome shape. Why should he *go away?* A sudden desperation made her feel sick. Had she really gone on knowing there was murder in his heart? Or was it just some fantasy, or nightmare, never touching reality! She started to tremble, her teeth chattering. Her silence had given consent, and her love had been so agonising as to prompt the silence which might hurtle them both into tragedy and destruction.

She looked a round her and everything seemed far away. These few years had been like living out of time, trapped by emotion in a vacuum. Was she a real person? Alive? What

day was it? What month? The silence was unearthly, the isolation greater than ever before,
yet she knew she was afraid to leave it and go
out into an unfamiliar world – alone. In the
past, the joy and happiness of the times she
and Melvin had been away together – the
memories – sustained her during the bleak
periods when he could visit her, but never
stay. She had seen so little of him recently. He
hadn't told her why. In fact what *had* he told
her? She clutched at memories. His promise
that she should have her brooch back, and
another to go with it… She heard the echo of
his voice, defiant and determined, when he
had said, *Mrs Ingram.* And just now…
Remember I love you. Why should she feel
this weight of depression? Whatever the
crime might be, she knew she must go on.
Carry out his orders. Of course he was right
not to want her in the district. She began to
buoy herself up, clinging to a little balloon of
happiness; a second of mental escape. But as
she caught sight of herself in the mirror, her
eyes looked back at her accusingly, and there
was no peace in her heart.

Distrust and suspicion took formidable
shapes. Suspicion about *what?* Why had he
not told her where he was going? The tiny
pinprick of doubt could not be denied…

The room had a sudden forlorn look, as
though emptied of furniture. The idea of
packing even a light suit case and getting

into Fowey filled her with dismay. Suit cases were associated with Melvin when they were going away together, and he had always looked after them. A London hotel on her own... Waiting – always waiting. And dreading what she might hear...

She went into the bedroom and sat down on the edge of the bed where they had lain together such a brief while before... The tears were running down her cheeks.

13

Carla realised that as she was spending a fortnight at Ascot, it meant that this was the last meeting with Adrian in what seemed an eternity. In addition, dread lay upon her like an ice block. No one could say that she would ever return to Polvose, and suddenly all its gloom, its haunting shadows, became doubly dear. All she asked was to have a short while in which to talk to Adrian.

She sat through the meal, eating mechanically, watching the candle-lit dining table through the blur of memory which took her to the cottage, and Gina. Would Melvin never stop talking? Would he go on and on about himself, as though he were the most exciting person in the world? Or was she jaundiced because she wanted to get out of the room, have coffee, and hope that Adrian would suggest that they went out into the grounds they both loved? He did exactly as she wished, and when they were walking along the familiar lawns, to her amazement he said, with an urgency that turned her gaze instantly to his, 'Carla, ours, I know, has been strange relationship – if you can call it that – but I need your help and–'

Instantly, she responded, with all the warmth that was inherent in her. 'Anything,' she said, spontaneously. 'Adrian, what is it?' Even in the dusk his face had a tinge of grey.

'Worry,' he replied.

For some intuitive reason, Carla did not attack the word.

'I think I share that,' she said gently, but without cynicism.

'They must not go to Paris tomorrow,' he said, with all the fervour, the passion, of which he was capable. 'I know you have great influence, and if you could use it–' He stopped, almost bereft of words.

Carla shivered as though she were part of the trembling light fading from the sky. Her voice was soft and gentle as she murmured, 'To prevent the holiday?'

'Yes.' He was quiet and sombre.

In a few seconds, Carla ran through the gamut of life, of emotion, finally to reach tenderness.

Adrian said bleakly, 'I have no influence with her – *you* could persuade *him*.'

Carla knew that this was not the time for argument. All she could give was sympathy. 'Something must have happened... Adrian – what?' She noticed how distraught he looked.

'I learned today that Melvin's first wife committed suicide.' He held her gaze with an inquiring look. 'Did you know that he had been married before?'

'Yes, because Vanessa told me, yesterday.'

'Did she mention suicide?'

'No.'

They looked at each other and Carla felt that all the breath had gone from her lungs. '*Suicide.*'

'I cannot imagine anyone more capable of driving Vanessa to suicide.' He added, 'Or having a better reason for wishing to do so.'

Carla refrained from comment. One day she would tell him the truth, but not now.

'There was a child that died when it was three months old. It was assumed that the shock was responsible for her taking her life.' He held Carla's gaze. 'Her body was found in the river.'

'Evidently the coroner was satisfied.'

'I wish I were. Yours is certainly a strange love.'

'We cannot choose where we love, Adrian, or there would never be heartache.'

'True,' he said ruefully. 'I must say that your case is the strangest I've ever come across. I find it incomprehensible – to use a very mild word.' He hurried on, 'But I'm getting away from the point. Will you use your influence?'

'I have very little to use. And you have to remember that Vanessa wants this trip more than anything in the world. I sometimes wonder if we haven't created a situation based on fear and anxiety.'

'Such as the window incident being our imagination? Don't try to make any excuses for him.' There was a grim look on Adrian's face. 'If anyone could murder a man, I could murder him.'

'In that case, you would murder his wife.'

'Your solicitude for her is touching.'

Carla felt what she believed to be his deep love and emotion, and his fury. There was a quietness within her, as though she might never see him again and could not bear to part in anger. 'My solicitude is genuine. More than that, I cannot say.' She looked at him and her eyes were gentle, almost appealing. 'Please believe me when I say that I would never destroy anything merely for my own happiness. I could not live with ruins around me. Whatever suffering surrounds this situation we – you and I – bear it in our respective ways.'

'And, of course, Perth did not destroy

anything – for Vanessa?'

'Of course it did and it has, also, made this trip to Paris doubly dear to her.'

Adrian was watching her as though trying to assess her knowledge. He shot the question, 'And you think that, in the circumstances, nothing should be done to prevent the holiday?'

'I think any efforts would be to no avail.'

'Not even your efforts?'

Carla managed to force a half smile. 'I could talk, cajole, plead – anything – but a man always, in the end, does what he wants.'

Adrian stared at her, amazed. She was the most incredible person he had ever met, and his love for her was rather like a hair shirt.

'And a woman?'

'Financial independence does the same. But,' her voice softened, 'I will speak to him about his first wife. I did not know anything about her.' As she spoke, she felt that being condemned by Adrian was far better than telling him the truth about Gina. She, Carla, could protect Vanessa; she could not be certain that Gina would be prepared to follow the example. She had every reason for doing the opposite.

Adrian said suddenly and irrelevantly, 'Carla, please get out of all this. Remain at Ascot.'

She stared at him in bewilderment, unable to fathom his meaning. She replied swiftly,

'Why do you not get out of it?'

He was stern. 'I am involved as a solicitor and a friend.'

'I,' she flashed back, 'am involved for my own reasons, and it would be useless to try to make you understand them. Surely this is off key? You ask me to use my influence with Melvin, and then suggest that I leave here altogether... Men always say they do not understand women, but if any woman can understand this complete change of attitude, she would be clairvoyant. The expression on his face made her add breathlessly, 'Adrian, is there something else?'

'Something I cannot tell you,' he said quietly. 'I wish to heaven I could.'

'Thank you for that trust, anyway.'

They both turned to look at the house, fascinated by its imposing and forceful façade. At that moment the afterglow flooded it with a light that became mystery. Carla wondered how any building could be both beautiful and sinister: how the perfect setting could breed such fear and unrest.

'I wish,' Adrian began.

'What?' Carla said in anticipation.

'Nothing: the less you know, the less you will have to worry about.' His gaze was gentle.

At that moment Vanessa came out of the house and joined them. She looked around her and said, 'I shall hate leaving this, even though I am so thrilled about tomorrow.' Carla noticed how her gaze met Adrian's. 'I think Cornwall has the magic of Pixies – perhaps an unreality, an escape, but so beautiful. Yet Paris will be so exciting. It is years since I was there.' She smiled from face to face. 'Bless you both for all you have done.'

Carla saw the expression on Adrian's face and she could read his thoughts. Here was a woman who felt instinctively that she would not see them again after that evening.

Adrian said – a note of humour in his voice – 'No speeches, by request.'

Vanessa laughed. In the evening light she had a serenity which enhanced her beauty.

Adrian was suddenly alert. 'What was that noise?'

Carla stiffened. 'Only the gulls.'

Vanessa sighed. 'I keep seeing so many shadows here that I've given up trying to fathom them.' She hastened, 'I promised Melvin I would bring you in. Some business matter he wants to talk over with you.'

'And,' thought Adrian bitterly, 'because he resents Carla being monopolised.'

It was a trivial thing that Melvin wished to discuss and could have waited until his return. Adrian delayed his going until the last moment; a premonition coming upon him like a black wave of depression. Yet, this of all nights Vanessa should be safe. Nevertheless, as he left the house he might have been alerted. He heard his name whispered and the solid black figure of Mrs Wells moved from a nearby spinney.

'Well?' He was in no mood to be patient. 'Do you have to creep about like this?' he added tensely.

'I creep about to – watch. There's something you ought to know. It's about Miss Selby and Mr Ingram.'

Adrian felt that he had been kicked just below the heart. 'I don't like gossip.'

'This isn't gossip. She is the woman in his life – the woman he stayed with in Perth. All I'm thinking about is Madam.'

It struck Adrian, even in that split second, just how curious human nature was. He had been saying exactly what Mrs Wells was now saying, but the words burned like a fire suddenly lit within him.

'What possible right – or proof – have you to make such a statement?'

'These,' she said quietly and handed him the brooch and the letter. 'I stole them from Miss Selby's room. They were concealed in a compartment of her suit case – the case she is taking with her tomorrow. And then there's the cottage.'

Adrian felt that the walls of the house were leaning down to catch every word, as the wind from the sea whined through the trees.

'Cottage,' he echoed.

'Down there,' she murmured, pointing in

213

the right direction. 'They meet there – secretly.' The beady eyes looked like hard black diamonds.

Pain, love, jealousy churned within Adrian. He did not underestimate Mrs Wells.

'And that's not all,' she went on. 'I found the panel that leads from Miss Selby's room to the grounds.'

Adrian's voice was cold, 'You've been very busy – haven't you?'

'My duty is to protect Madam.' She paused meaningfully. 'I thought I had better tell you these things first, before going to her.'

The moon slid from behind a cloud to reveal an expression both challenging and triumphant. 'We don't want Miss Selby back here.' She rustled the tissue paper in which the brooch was wrapped. It sounded as loud to Adrian as machine-gun fire. 'This is her brooch, but *she stole it* from Madam's room.'

'I should be careful what you say, Mrs Wells. The motive is important.'

'So, sir, is the evidence.'

Adrian spoke quietly. 'We agree on that, but, of course, you would have to prove how you came by it, and that it was Miss Selby's room from which *you* stole it.'

'We are not in a court of law.'

'It is always as well to assume that one is facing a jury before making any accusations.'

'I thought you'd give me good advice.

214

'I have.'

'And Madam?' The voice was not quite so sharp.

'Your silence will serve her best.'

'I don't want her to go tomorrow.' The words rushed out. 'I'd do anything – anything to stop her.'

The urgency communicated itself to Adrian in what he knew to be sincerity. 'I understand that,' he commented guardedly.

'I'm the only one who knows what he is. You mark my words, he'll drive her to suicide in the end.' She added viciously, 'Like he did his first wife. Madam doesn't know the truth about it all.'

'Then see that she doesn't know.'

'I'm sorry, sir, to have gone off like this. I don't as a rule.' She felt in a deep pocket which seemed to lie within yards of material and drew out a letter which she handed to him. 'I stole this, too,' she admitted. 'When you get into the light, you will see that it is from Paris – from the Grand Hotel. Miss Selby has booked in there for three weeks during the time Mr and Mrs Ingram are on holiday. Not, of course,' she said, 'at *their* hotel. But I will do as you say and keep quiet. Good night.' She vanished like a mysterious shadow lost in the background of trees.

Adrian's hands were trembling as he got into the car and read the letter. It confirmed what Mrs Wells had said. And he knew that all the characters in this grim charade were moving into position for the final tragedy.

He sat there looking on the scene around him with sightless eyes. All he could think of was Carla and not all the jealousy, the fear, or contempt, changed the love which seemed to increase with disillusionment.

14

Carla was awakened from fitful sleep, almost as though an unseen presence was in the room, and as she put out her hand to switch on the light, she felt the chill of terror lest another hand might touch hers, or some fearsome shape build up before her. But the room was empty, yet an awareness of something abnormal remained. She slid out of bed and flung on her house coat, still watchful and alert. Her first thought was Vanessa. Noiselessly, she went to Vanessa's room and opened the door without a sound. A shaft of moonlight fell upon Vanessa's face. Carla crept away, seeming to breathe for the first time. She reached the safety of her room, still tingling with apprehension and it was then, suddenly, her gaze became fixed on a panel in the wall – a panel open some inches. She put a hand to her mouth to stifle the cry that escaped her lips. Who was behind it? And if she dared to look, what would she see? She moved forward and grasped the edge as though it were a fire that would burn her. Even as her fingers touched the wood, the gap widened to reveal what, at first sight, appeared to be a dark chasm. Was Melvin lurking there, or could it be Gina? Was this the answer to her ability to get in and out of the house, as she had done?

Carla knew that she could not endure the suspense of conjecture. She must find out for herself. Swiftly, she stepped into a pair of slacks and pulled a jumper over her head, then with the aid of a torch began the descent down a steep staircase which turned and twisted so that anyone could lurk and be hidden in the shadows. Was that someone breathing? She stopped, petrified, imagination giving fear wings. No one was visible. The cool night air blew on her face as she neared the ground. Was it possible that this was a link with the cottage? All she knew was that it loomed eerie and menacing – if only by virtue of its secrecy. The thought struck her of how Melvin had reacted to the word, *explore*. And suddenly the blackness took on the ghostly blue tinge of moonlight playing on worn stone walls. With every step the mystery became more unbearable, the faintest sound like thunder. Finally she reached a heavy oak door and nerved herself to look back, finding the courage to flash the light of her torch to reveal what lay behind her – a steep staircase alive with a silence that became noise. The door was bolted and she realised that anyone could come after her and shut her out. Shaking, needing two hands and the clumsy manipulation of the torch, she managed to pull back the bolt... Now, her lungs seemed to be emptied of air and then almost bursting, as she left behind the last part of the terror. A few steps and she was in a copse. The moon filtered through the trees, etching pale shadows at her feet. But where now? It was a spot unknown to her and she stood helplessly, her fright almost greater than before. Then, thinking it must be a hallucination, her gaze focussed a pinpoint of light in the distance... It could only be from the house, and she walked towards it even though panic overwhelmed her at the possibility of having to retrace her steps. She stumbled breathlessly on, over the rough, uneven ground where bracken brushed frighteningly against her legs, making her increase her pace until, at last, the dark shadow of Polvose appeared to lift itself out of the density of trees closing in upon her. And all the time the light remained, finally leading her to a small, half-concealed door which seemed to be lower than the ground on which she was walking. She paused outside it, looking up at the house, trying to place the light in relation to the rest of the building. Moonlight made everything deceptive. Her torch revealed a key in the lock which she turned silently, cautiously, finding to her amazement that she was in the cloakroom adjoining Melvin's study. The door, as she shut it, merged into the structure inconspicuously. She knew the cloakroom and told herself that if Gina should be in the study, she would have no mercy for her.

This time she went into the room with confidence. The light was on and must have shone through a small circular window set almost at ceiling level. All was quiet, but she stood shivering with fear and exhaustion which dissolved into relief as she sank down in a nearby chair, closing her eyes and holding her head which throbbed. As she stirred, after a few seconds, and looked around her with greater perception, her gaze lowered and she saw a trickle of blood running beneath Melvin's desk to the stone fireplace.

'Oh God! *Vanessa!*' Her voice broke on a note of horror.

But when she reached the body behind the desk ... Melvin lay dead, and as she stood over him, Mrs Wells appeared from the hallway.

'I always knew you'd kill him,' she said quietly.

To Carla all that followed took the form of a nightmare. Vanessa's stunned disbelief, too great for tears: the tragic, mute appeal in her eyes.

Vanessa whispered, 'I was afraid – *I* was afraid and all the time–' She rushed on, 'Why doesn't Adrian come?' Her gaze focussed on Carla, it seemed almost with suspicion. 'Mrs Wells said you were in the study?'

'I was,' Carla agreed, and felt that she had water in her veins instead of blood.

'Why?'

Adrian arrived at that moment, coming into the house as though jet-propelled. Mrs Wells had been brief and to the point when she telephoned. But the word murder seemed to leap out at him like a monster.

Vanessa said, 'Thank God you're here… Oh, Adrian, what shall I do – what shall I *do*?'

'Just as I tell you,' he said firmly. 'I've already notified the police. They will be here at any moment.'

'But who could have done it?' Vanessa seemed to have shrunk to half her size. Her hair, ruffled from sleep, gave her a childish look which added to the poignancy of her utterances.

Mrs Wells said, 'We need not look far.'

Adrian ignored that. But dread lay upon him. He went into the study and made a few mental notes. By the time he returned to the hall a car drew up and Detective-Inspector Mayhew (whom Adrian knew very well) stood on the threshold as Adrian opened the door.

'Sorry about this, sir.'

'Bad business,' Adrian said. He led the way back to the study. His trained eye took in details which anyone else would overlook. 'A pretty hefty blow, delivered from strength,' he said, eyeing Adrian as he spoke. 'Apparently the murder weapon is missing.' He picked up the telephone and gave his orders. 'Now, I'd like to talk to the people who were in the house tonight.' The Inspector was a tall, square shouldered man, with a thin face and hawk-like eyes. Beneath a rather forbidding manner, there was an acceptance that human beings were not just names in a file to be dealt with as a computer dealt with facts. 'Mrs Ingram?'

Adrian said, 'Too shocked really to grasp it.'

The three women sat in silence as the two men entered the room which seemed to quiver with suspicion. Mrs Wells, militant, aggressive, had been determined not to leave her mistress alone with Carla.

After the first formalities were over, the Inspector asked the obvious question. Who discovered the body?

'I did,' Carla admitted and saw the look

which crossed Adrian's face.

'At what time would that be?'

'I suppose about three this morning.' She tried to keep her voice steady, and not to flinch before that searching gaze.

'Are you in the habit of roaming around the house at that hour, Miss Selby?'

'I have done so from time to time.'

The Inspector observed Carla's clothes and the mudstains on her stout shoes. 'Dressed as you are now?' The words were shot at her.

'Sometimes.'

Vanessa, white-faced, stricken, murmured, 'Carla.'

'I take it you also go *outside* the house and roam around,' he suggested, 'and that you did so tonight?'

'Yes.'

'Why?' His imperturbability seemed an accusation.

'Curiosity,' she replied with a certain defiance. 'I found a panel in my room open slightly and I went to explore where it led.'

'Really... Where did it lead?'

'Into the garden and to Mr Ingram's study.'

He nodded and Carla had the feeling that he did not believe a word she was saying.

'I'd like to see this panel.'

Carla murmured, 'Of course.'

The Inspector looked around him. 'Is there no one else in the house?'

'My husband,' Mrs Wells said instantly.

'Bring him here... Now, Miss Selby.'

They went up to Carla's room. 'But someone has shut it.' Carla walked to the spot, searching frantically to find out the secret of opening the panel. The Inspector followed her, running his fingers down the beading, pressing both lightly, and then with strength. He looked at Carla, 'This wall seems pretty solid to me.'

'But–' Carla made a gesture of despair. 'Mrs Ingram has always believed that there was a secret entry into this room.'

'I don't think we will pursue this any further.'

'Inspector,' Carla's voice held an urgency that arrested his attention. 'There is so much in this case; so much that could distress Mrs Ingram.'

'Whatever there is to discover, we shall discover. Murder is not a matter for discretion.'

They returned to the room and all eyes were upon them. Vanessa was huddled in her chair, her heart feeling that it dangled in an empty void... Melvin dead... She glanced at Carla half questioningly.

'The panel has been shut again,' Carla murmured.

'But,' Vanessa said instantly, and then stopped. So far as she knew only Melvin was in possession of its secret.

'Yes, Mrs Ingram?'

Vanessa hesitated, then, 'To my knowledge no one knew that there was a second entrance to that room.'

'Meaning that it had been a matter for discussion?' His voice was more gentle.

'In the sense that I mentioned to Miss Selby I had always felt there was some secret in connection with getting in, or out, of the room other than by the ordinary door. This is a very old house and one assumes things.' Her voice broke and tears welled into her eyes. 'Does it matter? My husband is dead – dead,' she repeated.

The Inspector spoke with feeling. 'I want to spare you as much as possible, Mrs Ingram. Sometimes the most trivial clue can lead one to the murderer.' He paused. 'You heard nothing unusual during the night?'

'No.' She hung her head as though ashamed. 'I slept… Mrs Wells awakened me and–'

Vanessa sat transfixed, she might have been a statue hewn from white marble.

'I don't think I need trouble you any more, Mrs Ingram,' the Inspector said sympathetically. 'I appreciate all you've been through. Believe me, everything will be done to find your husband's murderer.'

Adrian got to his feet. 'I will see you to your room.' He glanced at the Inspector, who nodded his approval. At the same time it registered: why should *Mr Grant* see Mrs Ingram to her room? He changed his attitude with the smoothness born of training. 'I think Mrs Wells should take care of Mrs Ingram.' He added beadily, 'And return here.' As he spoke he looked at Wells who sat quivering in his chair. Where did he fit into this picture? As a nonentity, or as a power of which no one was aware?

Carla absorbed every word spoken, but she felt that nothing around her was real. She recognised her own danger, and at the same time, felt it a fantasy. She looked at Adrian, feeling the pull of an emotion which had she known it tore at them both. Now, Vanessa was free, and when all the tumult, the tragedy, had died down, he would convince Vanessa that by marrying him she would have peace and security. In that second she could have changed the whole pattern, by confessing to a murder she had not committed... But it was not her nature to do so. The thought of Ascot and her parents strengthened her determination to prove her innocence, while knowing that, on circumstantial evidence, she must already be condemned, and even were this not so, Mrs Wells would make quite certain that she was accused.

A terror came over her as she saw Mrs Wells leading Vanessa out of the room – a Vanessa too stunned to realise who was accompanying her. In that moment she saw the window in her own room. Would Melvin, in death, still drive his wife to suicide? Carla said, her words hardly audible, 'Inspector, I don't know anything about this kind of procedure, but I beg of you to get one of your men to lock the door of my room.'

A steely gaze met hers. 'My men?'

'Yes, I heard them come almost immediately after your arrival.'

Adrian's voice held a note of such anxiety that the Inspector listened. 'There is a dangerous window in Miss Selby's room, and Mrs Ingram could easily *fall out of it.*' He added, 'I do not think you want a *suicide*, as well as a murder, on your hands.'

The Inspector got up, went out into the hall and spoke to the sergeant on duty. In a matter of minutes the key of Carla's room was in his hands.

Mrs Wells returned. She told the story of her relationship with Vanessa's family. Her sentences were brief, her tone calm, almost to the point of monotony. Her description of the events of the evening were factual.

The Inspector shot the question at her, 'And do you, also, roam about the house at night?'

'If things worry me – yes.'

'And you were worried last night?'

'Yes. I've never trusted Miss Selby.'

'I am not asking for your opinion,' the Inspector said curtly.

'But you want facts,' she flashed back. 'And the last one I can give you is that when I found Miss Selby standing over Mr Ingram's body, I said that I always knew she would kill him. She was jealous because of the holiday.' The beady eyes gleamed. 'She hated the idea of Mr Ingram going away with his wife.' She added swiftly, 'Miss Selby and Mr Ingram were lovers.'

'I see. Have you anything to say to that, Miss Selby?'

Carla saw the expression on Adrian's face and replied, 'Only that the statement is untrue.'

So much in this case that could distress Mrs Ingram.

The Inspector sighed. To get the truth would be a miracle. He switched to Adrian. 'When did you see Mr Ingram last?'

Adrian told him, and then continued, 'Miss Selby spoke of a secret panel in her room which we now know led finally to Mr Ingram's study. Wouldn't it be a good idea to work backwards from the study and see what you find?'

'Thank you, Mr Grant,' came the cynical reply, 'but I do not need to be taught my job... Now–' He looked at Wells whose face was almost a death mask. 'Where were you during this time – wandering about, too?' he added impatiently. 'And don't look at your wife. I'm addressing you.'

A malevolent expression crept over Wells' face. 'I was asleep. But I heard a noise and voices.'

'You mean you were awakened by the noise and voices.'

'I suppose that was it.'

'Did you notice the time?' The Inspector prayed for one thread of information to be pulled out of disorder.

'Yes, it was about half past two. Never can tell exactly with these illuminated clocks.'

'What was your relationship with your master?'

'Not good, not bad.' He added, 'I did my job and kept out of the way most times.'

'And you did not leave the house?'

'Not me; too ghostly-like around these parts.' He shot a furtive glance at his wife who was sitting upright in her chair, hands clasped in her ample lap. A faint sneer touched her lips, but she was thankful that nothing had been betrayed.

But just as Wells relaxed, thinking no more would be asked of him, the Inspector rapped out, 'How do you mean "ghostly-like"?'

Wells was far more afraid of his wife than the Inspector. He stammered, 'Always seeing things that are not there.'

'Or people, perhaps?'

'That's right.' He was getting bolder.

'Do you know anything about this secret passage?'

Mrs Wells' square body sagged a little. The flash of fear in her eyes did not fail to register with the Inspector.

'Yes.'

'Then why didn't you say so?'

'You didn't ask me.'

'Now I am.'

'The Master often used it.'

'When?'

'Sometimes days, sometimes nights.'

Carla listened mechanically, her gaze wandering to Adrian, looking for some sign that might give her understanding, but he was the solicitor intent only on the words being uttered, and when he did catch her eye, his expression was baffled.

'Come back to the noise and voices you heard.' The Inspector decided that if there was a person in that room from whom he might obtain one workable clue, this was the man.

Wells looked confused. 'Well, sir, I mean I was half asleep, as you might say–'

'But you do recall the time?' There was nothing aggressive in the Inspector's manner, just a tinge of authority.

'Yes.'

'Then try to recall what sort of noise it was and if the voices were angry–'

The room seemed to tremble with the silence that fell in it.

'Well, sir, my room is above the study and

I couldn't have been woken except by angry voices.'

Carla tensed, every nerve on edge.

'But you could not recognise those voices?'

'Not on oath, sir – except that I would say a man and a woman were quarrelling. It was a kind of scrambled sound and I was sleepy; I went back to sleep.'

The Inspector wished that he could. 'Have you ever heard that noise before?'

'Never.'

The Inspector nodded.

Mrs Wells, while still sitting upright, allowed herself the comfort of dropping her shoulders an inch or two.

There were no more questions asked but, apart from Adrian, the others in the room were warned not to leave the house.

And by this time, the house and grounds were encircled by vigilant police. Inside, the police doctor, fingerprint experts, local Press photographers, had moved in.

Carla had a matter of seconds to speak to Adrian alone, but it was he who spoke first. 'You may need a solicitor, Carla. May I suggest Clark?'

'So you think I'm a murderess?' She managed to keep emotion out of her voice.

'The police may have that idea,' he replied.

15

Carla, awakening after two or three hours of sleep, thought how in tragedy, triviality obtrudes. Her mind was rather like a Hoover collecting dust. That she was a suspect left her strangely indifferent. She tried to recall all that Gina had said to her... *Gina.* It was also strange that, while at the back of her mind, Gina had been of such concern, she had almost overlooked her in the tension that made rational assessment impossible. *Gina!* The name re-echoed. It was rather like looking at a friend and admiring, or criticising – mentally – without saying one word. Was she still at the cottage? If not, where was she? Carla knew that she must find her way to the cottage despite the police.

The morning light flooded her room and Mrs Wells brought in the tea with incredible aplomb. Carla felt that she would make an excellent wardress in a prison – and that was doing the wardresses a great injustice.

The house might well have been a prison, and its occupants prisoners. Unless they behaved normally – according to pattern – life would be impossible.

'Mrs Ingram?' Carla asked and the name

was a question.

'I saw to it that she had a long sleep. She is not yet awake.'

Carla felt that throughout the rest of her life she would always see Mrs Wells as a large, dark blind. *Throughout the rest of her life.* The words suddenly had significance. If circumstantial evidence could prove her guilty of murder ... would there be any life? She could not remember all the absurdities of the law. Imprisoned for life. Hanged. One fact stood out in her mind: she was not going to allow this woman to defeat her without a fight.

Suddenly, Carla heard her name called in panic and she rushed out of bed into Vanessa's room, shut, and locked, the door.

Vanessa was sitting up in bed, looking like a doll from which the face had been stripped of its paint. 'I slept and he is dead,' she cried. Her eyes seemed to hold the tragedy of the world. 'Oh, Carla – help me.'

Carla soothed her as a mother soothes a child. 'You needed sleep.' At that moment, Carla thought of Ophelia. Would this drive Vanessa mad?

'You won't leave me – promise you will not leave me?' There was a dazed look in her eyes and then suddenly, with the aggressiveness of a tiger, she asked, 'You did not kill him – did you? I could not bear it if you killed him.'

232

Carla's gaze was almost mesmeric. 'I swear on oath that I did not kill him.'

'But I had said so many things – so many things,' she whispered.

'We all say things.'

Vanessa nodded, comforted. Then, 'I've been thinking of that woman and of seeing someone in the house...'

Carla said with authority, 'You just rest and leave things to me.'

'I'm frightened of Mrs Wells.' Vanessa shook her head. 'She is good and kind, but ... I cannot explain... Carla, tell me please, what was that secret passage like... I know now that Melvin used it. It wasn't only *the window* in your room.' Her voice broke. 'No matter what I feel now, does not alter the past... But we were going to be happy... I felt like a child looking at a Christmas tree.' She bowed her head and sobbed. 'Oh, Carla ... I'll never *see* him again. That is the most dreadful part.'

Carla listened, her thoughts both with Vanessa and Adrian. Soon the story of the murder would be in all the papers. Murder at Polvose. She must get through to her parents before they read about it. When Vanessa was calmer she went downstairs. A police officer stood in the hall doorway and the full impact of the tragedy – with its complications – came upon her. He turned at the sound of footsteps. She explained her mission, meeting his gaze with a steady courage. He nodded his sanction. The telephone lines were taken care of, anyway.

Adrian arrived about three minutes after the Inspector that morning. Still no murder weapon had been found, and the search was going on meticulously and painstakingly. The house had never seemed more uncanny or so unreal. Reality always drained the drama from the events of magnitude in life – perhaps it was a fact which nature conceded to the sufferers. The shock came later.

Everyone in the house was questioned again – this time singly.

Adrian managed to speak to Carla before her turn came. 'Is there anything – *anything* you can think of about last night?' He spoke swiftly. 'Or any other nights. The shadow – the figure – in your bedroom when we stood together on the lawn. Have you any *idea*–'

Carla said urgently, thinking of Gina, 'Will you do one thing for me – for Vanessa, if you like.'

'Name it.' He tried to keep his voice controlled.

'You can move freely. Go to the cottage and see what you can find.'

He was grave instead of cynical. 'Retrieve your possessions?'

Carla met his gaze very steadily. 'You will probably know a great deal more when you get there. I was intending to go–'

'It would be madness to try,' he rapped out. 'Not that you would get further than the grounds.'

'Suspect number one, in fact.'

He studied her with a puzzled contemplation. 'In any case I will do what you ask... Carla–'

The Inspector called Carla into the morning-room at that moment. She faced him without flinching.

'I'd like to know exactly what you saw when you went into the study last night. You were obviously familiar with the surroundings.'

'Yes.'

'And having reached the copse you found your way there by instinct, I presume.' His words were crisp, his eyes so watchful that they were unnerving.

Carla breathed deeply. 'Never having been that way before, there was no question of instinct. There was a light in the distance. I walked – or stumbled would be a better word – towards it.'

He stared at her, lowered his head for a second and then raised it quickly. 'Having lived here you must have been able to place that light, surely. To know, in fact, just where you were going.'

'I had no idea where the light would lead, except that I assumed it must bring me to Polvose.'

'And you couldn't place the position of the light in relationship to the house?' His voice was hard.

'No.'

'But the light was on in the study when you entered it.'

'Yes.' She gave him stare for stare. 'And if you look at the position of that small window almost at ceiling level – look at it carefully–'

'Which you did on entering the room?'

'Yes. It is on the left of the room and while I was guided by it in the darkness, I realised it had not been straight ahead, but *to* the left.'

'And this you worked out afterwards.'

'I realised it, Inspector.'

'Go on; you entered the study, found the position of the light... What then?'

'I flopped down in the nearest chair and held my head in my hands. It hadn't been a particularly restful time.'

He eyed her and it was impossible to fathom what was going through his mind. All she knew was the fact that he was trying to trap her.

'So you didn't see the body on entering the room?'

'No... The first thing I noticed when I had got my breath, if you like, was a trickle of blood running from the side of the desk to the fireplace.' She hesitated. Should she mention the terror of thinking it was Vanessa? She decided against it.

'Well?' What was she hiding? 'So you were sitting down when you saw the trickle of blood?'

Carla drew a hand across her forehead. 'Yes, I'd opened my eyes and looked down. When I reached the front of the desk ... I saw Mr Ingram lying there. It was horrible.'

'But you didn't call out?' He added swiftly, 'I should have thought that would have been natural.'

'I cried, "Oh God..." but Mrs Wells opened the door when I'd only just had time to realise who was lying there.' She added, with spirit, 'And I can remember her words, Inspector, "I always knew you'd kill him."'

The Inspector pursed his lips.

'So you confirm what she said on this point.'

'Yes.'

'Tell me,' he asked with a sudden change of tactics. 'Who else in the house could you have imagined being murdered?'

'I did not use the word *murdered*, Inspector, I spoke of *who was lying there*.'

'And when you saw the trickle of blood you did not automatically think in terms of murder?'

'Blood does not rule out injury, fainting,' she replied. 'One's thoughts at a time like that are impossible to define.'

'And what was your relationship with the murdered man?' His eyes were full of suspicion.

'I hadn't a relationship with Mr Ingram.'

'Just an employer?'

'I was engaged by Mrs Ingram.'

'Yet you were on Christian-name terms.' The voice hardened. 'Come, Miss Selby.'

Carla felt anger rising and knew she must curb it. 'Being on Christian-name terms means very little today.'

He swung away from the subject. 'And you can't remember any details about the murder? Seeing any weapon of any kind?'

'I hardly had time to see the body before Mrs Wells appeared,' Carla replied swiftly.

For a second she felt that she had made her point. Then suddenly, shatteringly, he asked, 'If, as you say, your relationship with the murdered man was purely platonic, why had you booked in at an hotel in Paris for the last three weeks of the time that he and his wife were due there?'

Carla gave a disbelieving gasp. 'Booked in – but I've not done any such thing.' She cried, 'Inspector, please believe me. I'm going to – was going to – stay with my parents. Why should I want to go to Paris?'

'That is precisely what I am asking you,' he said with authority.

Carla shivered. Her gesture was helpless. 'I can do no more than tell you again what I

238

just now said. Am I allowed to ask the source of your information?'

'No. I shall want to see you again.'

'I can add nothing to what I've already told you.'

He looked at her with a strange intensity. 'It is not what you've told me, Miss Selby, but what you have avoided telling me that matters.'

Carla's voice was faintly cynical as she asked, 'Then am I allowed to know at which hotel I was supposed to be staying?'

'When I've completed my inquiries,' he replied. 'That will be all for now. If you can remember any details that might be of help, let me know – in your own interest. This, I assure you, does not give me pleasure. If you are not guilty then your silence can be helping the very person we are searching for.' His expression was grimly determined. 'And we shall not fail.' He shot the final question at her, 'Can you give any reason why Mrs Wells should have used the words she did last night, unless she had some evidence to support them?'

Carla met his gaze very levelly. 'Only resentment of my being in the house.'

'I see.'

He left and joined the zealous team searching every inch of the ground for any clues that might be of help. There was no trace of the weapon which had killed Melvin, and while the study had been the scene of immense activity, it would appear that nothing of importance had been discovered.

The house took to itself its own private silence of death. The pathetic suit cases, with only last-minute items to be packed, looked like faces without eyes – discarded and as empty as loneliness.

Vanessa sat staring out over the garden. Looking at her, Carla thought that she might have already gone on into another world. And in this knowledge her own vigilance increased – to prevent the second tragedy. Even Mrs Wells became subdued.

16

The murder at Polvose made headlines in the newspapers the following morning. A distinguished man, living in one of the most beautiful parts of Cornwall. The reporters did their best to make truth sound stranger than fiction. Nevertheless, the grim, sordid details, they knew, would eventually be revealed. They had the material for a garment – but not the garment itself.

Carla lived on a razor edge, as she waited for Adrian to come to see her. Until he had been to the cottage, she felt – rightly, or wrongly – that she could not mention Gina's name. What might he find there?

He came back to Polvose in the late afternoon of the day following Melvin's murder. Vanessa was in her room, trying to rest because Doctor Mills (whom Mrs Wells had taken upon herself to call in) insisted that it was necessary. Having been shut off from Polvose, because of Melvin's prejudice, he was both gentle and understanding. He had always regarded Vanessa with great respect.

Carla looked at Adrian as he came into the room. Her expression was one of anticipation. He must have explored the cottage and now she could tell him the truth. But the atmosphere was like a deep freeze as he said, 'I have fulfilled my bargain.' As he spoke he opened his brief case and handed her a dress, a cardigan, a nightdress, a négligé and a compact. 'I believe these are yours,' he said, in a tone that made him a stranger.

Carla stared at them, her skin feeling that it had lifted itself from her flesh. She knew that he was right, but she asked quietly, 'And have you ever seen a nightdress of mine, or a négligé?'

'That was Melvin's privilege. But your expression was proof of ownership… Also, it so happened that I was there when Melvin gave you this compact on his return from Paris.'

'That is true.' She realised that nothing

241

she could say would sound valid. 'And the things you have there do belong to me.'

'I will return the compact, but it would be dangerous to leave these things with you.'

'Dangerous?'

'We might as well be on radar.'

'What else did you find at the cottage?' Now she realised that Gina was behind all this. *She* had taken these possessions and left them as evidence.

'Nothing,' he said coldly.

Carla shivered. 'But there must have been–'

'What?' He sounded like the Inspector.

'Other personal possessions.' Her voice was breathless. *'Nothing!* Do you mean that the furniture has gone?'

'I mean that only the furniture and these things were left.' He paused for a second. 'Oh, one other thing – your photograph.' As he spoke, he handed it to her.

It was an old photograph, in miniature. Carla could not identify herself, but she knew that she had packed it – with many other little mementoes – reminding her of her happy childhood days, and the delight that had accompanied her adolescence.

'I suppose,' she said honestly, 'that I must have looked like that. All I know is, that I did pack it' – her voice broke – 'and giggled at how I looked.'

Adrian's expression was inscrutable. 'Now

you have it back – all the things back.'

'In your keeping,' she said doubtfully.

'For your benefit… How did you get on with the Inspector this morning?'

Carla felt that she had been put through a washing machine, and was still mentally whirling. 'He distrusts me… I did not mention that we were all afraid that Vanessa would be murdered.'

'So that, apart from the murder, he knew you were concealing something. Naturally, he distrusts you.'

She shook her head in a little despairing gesture. Then, 'Is it possible you can ignore Mrs Wells in your calculations?'

Adrian took out his cigarette case and lit a cigarette.

'All right, Carla. Shall we leave it at that?'

'By all means,' she retorted. 'Thank you for retrieving the evidence for me. I appreciate it, but I am certain that you must be deriving great satisfaction because your theory about Melvin and I having been lovers has proved correct.' Her voice trembled. 'I must be singularly lacking in emotion not to be mourning him now. Or had that not struck you?'

His expression was inscrutable as he answered, 'It has not been overlooked, but, then, lovers have been known to quarrel and hate where they once loved – particularly when there was a wife in the picture.' He looked suddenly grave. 'Only the truth can help you,' he said with urgency.

'When you accept my word and trust me, I will give you truth.' She moved away towards the door. 'Are you going to say anything about the nightmare we've lived through concerning Vanessa?'

'No.' The reply was immediate. 'It could serve no good purpose and cause Vanessa greater distress.'

Carla as in all moments of crisis recalled the most irrelevant things. In her case it was the original advertisement which had brought her to Polvose. *Adventurous type wanted.* And then the words of the rugged-faced Cornishman who had said, 'Ingram! Ah that be in woods, near creek. Trespassers – they be forbid.'

'I'd like to talk to Clark. The Inspector will be back to see me again and I need advice.'

Adrian inclined his head in a gesture of agreement. 'I warn you, Clark does not take kindly to lies.'

'He will not get them any more than he will judge me.' Her voice held a note of weariness. 'I will telephone him.' And all the time she spoke one part of her brain thought of Gina. Where was she? Conjecture was impossible, but remembering her desperation Carla felt that she, above all, had reason to murder Melvin once she discovered about Paris. *Paris.* 'Adrian–' The utterance of his name revived an intimacy.

'Yes.' He waited.

She tried to keep emotion out of her voice. 'Have you heard that I was due to go to Paris and had booked in at an hotel during the time they were to be there?'

'Yes.'

'From whom?'

'I cannot answer that question. Jumping to conclusions can be fatal.' His voice was quiet. 'The Inspector knew, of course?'

'Yes. I–'

'What?' There was a sudden anxiety in his attitude.

'Nothing that would interest you.' She reached the door and was gone before he had time to open it.

Mrs Wells darted out of sight, having tried to overhear what was being said, then she turned her back, her expression a mixture of triumph and hostility. 'You certainly didn't leave any clues in the study – no finger-prints, even. But your timing was wrong...'

Carla experienced fear – a shuddering fear – for the first time. *Circumstantial evidence.* It was building up around her to a degree which made every word she uttered suspect. She faced Mrs Wells squarely. Her voice was cool and held significance. 'Yours was perfect. I am sure you do not usually stand outside the study door in the early hours of the morning, unless you have good reason for doing so. *You* would never leave finger-prints.'

For the first time, she saw that mask-like face betray terror. 'Are you daring to suggest that I–'

'Go on, Mrs Wells.'

The silence came down threateningly. Carla added, 'I will finish your sentence ... that you murdered Mr Ingram.'

17

Looking at Vanessa, Carla thought how much more kindly grief was than the conflict of loving the wrong man. Even Melvin, in death, would seem to Vanessa to be imbued with qualities he did not possess, and she would hug to her heart the knowledge of that final understanding and the memory of a holiday which they had planned together – even though tragedy wiped it out.

The platitude of *time* could not fail to be valid. Vanessa was too young not, eventually, to enjoy life again. Adrian would ease her back to normality, love her, and give her ultimate happiness.

Carla thought that she, herself, might take refuge in some hope for the future – assuming she had one – but the raw wound in her heart at that moment was unbearable. She turned her gaze towards grounds she had come to love. The fair summer day was so gentle; the house so tragic.

Vanessa said suddenly, 'Carla, I've just realised that when I spoke to the Inspector this morning' – she could not bring herself to mention last night – 'I forgot about my feelings that, recently, I thought I saw someone in the house. So many shadows. I mentioned it all to you.' She sighed deeply. 'One cannot remember all the things. My mind is blank, because I cannot believe this is happening.'

Carla tried to be detached in order to be helpful. 'The Inspector will realise that.'

'What enemies had Melvin?' It was a plaintive cry. 'I've tried to think … could it be that woman? He said it was all over. She might have had other ideas. But how could she get *in*? Unless through your room.'

Carla tried to sound calm. 'As I found that outlet too late, no one can say.' A sickening fear made Carla cold. Was Vanessa really suspecting her – subtly prompted by Mrs Wells? It would be a death of ignominy to be despised by Vanessa, and condemned as Melvin's mistress. 'I should know if there had been anyone in the room. I am not a heavy sleeper – at least not since I came here.'

'Poor Carla, I have dragged you into so much.'

'I could have left here.'

'But you stayed.'

'And shall remain, as I promised, until everything around you is quiet.'

'In my misery, I am very lucky... Adrian has been wonderful. Taking over all the formalities–' The tears rolled unchecked down her face. 'Oh Carla! It is all so strange ... love, life – everything. And after all the suffering, the fear– I'd give my own life to have him back.' She added wistfully, 'And that would not be any good.' Her voice broke. 'I must not break down. I couldn't bear that. Yet it is like living with spikes in my heart.'

Carla brushed a hand across her eyes. 'You have been so brave. I am not sure I could have faced up to things–'

'I think it is afterwards – later – that one realises... So much to do and to think about now... The Inspector was kind.'

It struck Carla, then, what sudden death – either by murder, accident, or physical causes – meant. And even though she despised Melvin, the house was no more peaceful without him. Was it his shadow lingering over them all? Was he saying, 'They shall never be free of me'?

Adrian returned again to see them at five o'clock. Carla said to him, 'Now you are here and can stay with Vanessa, I want to go into St Austell.'

'What for?' He did his best to conceal his anxiety.

'I hardly think it would interest you ... just so long as you are with Vanessa – that is important.'

Carla drove to St Austell, wishing that Fowey had a Detective-Inspector, instead of a Sergeant-in-Charge. She was quite prepared to find that her journey was futile, but Detective-Inspector Mayhew was available. She was shown into his office and said, coming immediately to the point, 'Inspector, you said that if I could remember any details that might be of help, to let you know... That is the purpose of this visit.'

'I'm grateful, Miss Selby.'

'I know that I am in no position to tell you what to do–' Her gaze was so challenging that he could not ignore it. 'If you could double your guard between my bedroom and the late Mr Ingram's study, you will have your murderer.'

He looked at her with a calm, doubting expression. 'We listen to everything.'

Carla said boldly, 'I am not under arrest and I have not been called here for questioning. But–'

'What?' He interrupted with the skill associated with his job.

'Otherwise you will be investigating *my* murder.'

'And what brings you to that conclusion?'

'You are the detective – not I. But I do know that I am entitled to police protection. That is what I am asking for tonight.'

Mentally, he gave her a mark. 'Tell me, Miss Selby, why did you go to Polvose in the beginning?'

'Because I wanted to get away from dreary tycoons.' Carla gave a half smile. 'But you will have, by now, all the details of my life.' She got up. 'I do not want to waste your time, but *two people* will use that secret passage to my room tonight. I am prepared to take the risk of being in the room. All I ask is that you give me some protection. You want to tie up this murder, I presume.' Carla added, 'And if your police hordes have not the secret between my room and the study by now ... you will never find it.'

After Carla had gone, the Inspector got on to his minnows. Miss Selby was a woman to be reckoned with – guilty or not guilty.

That night Polvose seemed to lie in the shadow of a tiger waiting to pounce. Everything that Carla had loved about it was magnified – as were her fears. She had talked to Clark and put her burden on his shoulders, thankful for his understanding. Adrian was there, keeping vigil and, she knew, watching her like a cat a mouse. She walked with him in the garden overlooking the creek, and where her window seemed to be a beacon – unlit and yet at the point of flame.

The warm sensuous night held an enthral-
ment which bore no relationship to any
particularly country, and yet had a simplicity
which made the moon seem brighter, and
the cool darkness an emotion.

'How long are you staying here … it is
late,' she spoke tritely.

'All night,' he replied, 'should I be
needed.' His gaze took in the scene around
them and his heart felt like lead. 'The police
are swarming here,' he said abruptly.

'Watching me.' She spoke lightly. 'Inci-
dentally, Clark had more faith in me than
you… Forgive me, I'm going to bed; I'm
very tired.'

Carla went upstairs with Vanessa who
leaned on her heavily. She might have been
an old woman. They parted at their respective rooms.

'If you need me,' Carla said.

Vanessa shook her head. 'The tablets Doctor gave me knock me out. They are the
same that Mrs Wells must have kept after I
had been very ill – only once – since we came
here.' She paused. 'I wish I did not have to
wake up, Carla. You don't know how I wish
it.'

Carla undressed, had a second bath
(facetiously telling herself that should she be
murdered she would be doubly clean), and
got into bed. Once the light was out the eerie
sensation made her tense and alert. It was

the unknown that terrified her. Her skin was damp, her heart seemed to be thumping against the bed. Her gaze, in the moonlit darkness (she had left a chink in the curtains open at the deadly window), was focussed upon the panel, and the greater her concentration, the more confused she became. Was it this one, or that? She was exhausted and drowsy with sleep, her eyelids felt that they had lead weights upon them... She *must* not sleep... She must keep awake.

And then she saw the panel move... Rigid, every pore in her body iced.

Gina slid through.

So she did know how to enter the room. 'He's dead,' she murmured. 'Dead.'

Carla switched on the light.

'They were going away together – to Paris. I read it in the papers.' She looked like a pale tulip denied water. 'You must have known that night when you came to see me.'

'I do not have to give you reasons, or explanations,' Carla said quietly.

'But you are human... I believed him. I *believed* him.'

It was the cry of women through generations. Carla thought, even in that second, that to a man, silence prevented a lie, and a half truth constituted *truth*.

'You must have been here before? This was your method of entry?'

Gina sank down on the edge of the bottom

of the bed. 'Yes.' Her head was bowed. 'You see,' she said almost childishly, 'I had to *know*. He told me to go to London–'

Carla was suspicious. 'And did you go?'

'No. You don't understand.'

Carla hardened her heart to the cry.

'No one ever understands... This is murder.'

'You believe–'

'I neither believe, nor know, anything.' Carla hated every second of this. 'You chose your life, now you have to face the consequences.'

'Meaning that you have told the police about me?'

Carla shook her head. 'I have never mentioned your name, but don't underestimate the police. I told them that I should have two people here tonight. You are the first.'

'And the second?' Gina said immediately, 'Mrs Wells. *She* killed him.'

'Were you a witness?'

Carla wondered just how far the police were away.

'I could not have been a witness unless I had been there.'

'Exactly,' Carla said. 'This is your problem, not mine.' Then, 'Who saw you come in here?'

'No one, as far as I know, but the trees make it difficult to tell.'

'I hope,' Carla said, 'that they take care of

you on the way out.'

'You think I murdered him – don't you?'

'I do not even *begin* to think any more.'

Gina got up from the bed. 'It doesn't matter, anyway,' she said.

The panel closed. Carla lay there, every instinct longing to call out. She knew that Gina would be stopped as she left the house. *Knew*. Why should she know? Gina had been allowed in, therefore the Inspector could not have taken seriously anything that she, herself, had told him. Why had Gina cleared the cottage and yet not been away? Her tragic innocent pose could be her finest deception.

How still everything had become. No breeze stirred the trees; no owl hooted. All the time she watched the panel, as though awaiting a monster. At last, restless, she got up and put on a warm house-coat. The bed seemed to take on the shape of a coffin. And now there was no sleep in her eyes.

The window beckoned her and she moved towards it. The beauty and grandeur of the creek below, moonlit, seemed to hold the secret of eternity. And although she gazed, she did not lose sight of the panel.

Suddenly, her attention was diverted to the door which began to open slowly, without anyone about to enter being visible. Carla watched. And that dark shape came into the room, a tray and a glass of milk in her hand.

'I've brought you–' Mrs Wells' voice faltered as she looked at her empty bed. 'Miss Selby.'

'I'm here,' Carla managed to say, trying to keep the terror from her voice.

'Ah ... such a perfect night. And no police about for a change.'

The words held dread.

'You thought I'd be stupid enough to come from *there* – didn't you?' She indicated the panel as she spoke. 'You're going out of the window meant for her, and then there'll be peace in this house.' As she spoke she moved forward, having put the tray down on a table nearby.

Carla tried to scream, but the muscles of her throat seemed paralysed. As were her limbs. In that split second, she realised that her suicide would be a confession of murder, and this woman would go free. She managed to get away from the window, but not far enough away, before her legs refused to support her. And in that second, the voice of the Inspector said, 'Don't worry, Miss Selby.'

And all Carla could say was, 'You believed me – you *believed* me.'

'My men do not need to be seen in order to be here. I want you to awaken Mrs Ingram, and then come downstairs. We have your other nocturnal visitor under guard.' He looked at Mrs Wells and then at the police officer standing in the doorway. Mrs

Wells was led away.

'Must I wake Mrs Ingram?'

'She is entitled to be there when I make the arrest,' he said quietly.

Vanessa was trance-like as she and Carla went into the sitting-room. Investigations. What did they matter? She was suddenly alone – frighteningly alone. In life Melvin could reduce her to a state of misery which had often made her long for death. Yet, without him, what lay ahead? She had become resigned to suffering – it seemed normality. Happiness was foreign.

'Now, Miss Clements,' the Inspector began. 'Suppose you tell us why you came here tonight.'

Gina sat, hands drooping in her lap, as though all strength had gone out of them. And when it came to the test, she hated having to hurt the woman who had been no better treated than she. She told her story briefly, her voice expressionless.

'Have you ever met Mrs Ingram?'

'No.'

'How long were you Mr Ingram's mistress?'

'For five years.'

Vanessa gave a little cry.

'I'm sorry, Mrs Ingram, this isn't pleasant... Did you know of your husband's infidelity?'

'Yes.'

'And that it was with Miss Clements?'

'No.'

Adrian looked at Carla and suddenly amid all the macabre proceedings suspicion died. Together they hung on every word being uttered and Carla found herself praying that Gina might not be guilty. Surely, since the police had witnessed the scene with Mrs Wells, there was no need for this.

'But *you* knew, Mrs Wells.' The Inspector looked grimly accusing. 'Why direct your venom towards Miss Selby?'

'She was more dangerous.'

'In what way?'

'Miss Clements didn't come into the house – live in it.'

'Ah, but Miss Clements has been seen in it. I suggest by you.'

'I could not have identified her,' Mrs Wells said archly.

'Did you see her here on the night of the murder?'

'Yes.'

'Where?'

'Coming out of the study.'

'Why didn't you mention this before?' His voice was like flint grating on jagged stone.

'I didn't want Madam to know.' She added in a burst of passion, 'She had been so happy about going to Paris.'

'I see. I suggest, Mrs Wells, that very little you have said about this case is true. And that you hated Mr Ingram.'

'No.'

'And that was why you killed him. And if you could have committed your second crime, Miss Selby's death would have appeared evidence of her guilt.'

The silence that fell for a second seemed to bring with it the heat of a desert.

'I do not have to answer that question.' The words were uttered almost defiantly. 'When *you* get sufficient evidence to arrest me, I will talk.' She looked towards Gina. 'If you want your perfect motive, you will find it there. The discarded mistress.' Her eyes had a fire in them as she added, 'Mr Ingram would never have been satisfied with just *one* woman as well as his wife. Miss Selby was far more important to him.'

Gina's head was bowed; her face like death. She said, her voice hardly audible, 'I was in the house, as Mrs Wells has stated.'

'For what reason?'

'Suspicion – distrust. I wanted to see for myself.' She looked at Carla, half apologetically. 'I saw Mrs Wells coming out of the study. She looked pale and she had something wrapped in brown paper under her arm. I was scared and I ran away.'

'Not using your usual method of entry,' the Inspector said with a touch of cynicism.

'No… And I saw' – she glanced at Wells – 'him.'

Wells cried out. 'That isn't true. I was in bed I told you, Inspector.'

The Inspector said fiercely, 'Everyone tells me something and I have to sort out ten per cent of truth against ninety per cent of lies. All I can say is that this place must have been like the maze at Hampton Court.' He stopped abruptly, then, 'Mrs Ingram, can you remember if your telephone was on transfer that night?'

Vanessa did not hesitate. 'No it wasn't, Inspector.'

'Are you quite sure of that?'

'Quite sure. As we were–' Her voice broke as she uttered the 'we were' – 'going away in the morning, we kept it on normal service.'

He nodded and looked at Mrs Wells, who said immediately, 'I remember that, too.'

'Do you usually deal with the transfer-restore calls?'

'No, Madam always does.'

The Inspector looked from face to face and his expression sent a shudder over Carla. The room became airless, the tension mounted as, turning to Vanessa, he said quietly, '*You murdered your husband*, Mrs Ingram, and I must warn you that anything you say will be taken down in evidence.'

Carla cried out, 'No; no!'

Vanessa's voice seemed to come from a great distance. 'Yes, Inspector. I murdered him.'

Mrs Wells pleaded. 'She doesn't know what she is saying, she—'

'But I do,' the Inspector said curtly. He looked at Vanessa. 'Your telephone *was* on transfer that night ... I checked with the telephone people. You could not have realised that they have a time check on that service.'

Vanessa shook her head. 'It did not occur to me; I wanted the telephone cut off as a precaution.'

Carla and Adrian had no words to utter. They could only look at each other in mute appeal.

Vanessa said: 'I'd like to explain, In-spector... You see my husband was a schizo-phrenic. When I married him I knew he had been in a mental home under treatment. I also knew that he had been married before and that his wife was dead. He said it was because their daughter died when she was three months old. I didn't question him, but I always felt that there was something more than that. I learned later that she had taken her life.' She glanced at Adrian. 'I've always felt that you knew about it. In fact, I felt that you were the one person who suspected me all along.' An expression touched her face, making it beautiful. 'I knew before Carla came here that Melvin was getting worse and that I loved him enough to kill him rather than that he should go back into a home. I worked it out so that it would seem an accident – that was why I wanted to go away with him... I built up the story about his intention to murder me to divert suspicion.' She looked at Carla apologetically. 'No one could have said what he might do.'

Gina cried, 'Oh God.'

'I knew about you,' Vanessa said quietly, 'although I denied it just now. I knew about the cottage. I pretended to you, Carla, because I needed your help. It was wrong and weak. But he really murdered me a long time ago. Yet he could not leave me because he needed me. His life was a hurt and I was the only one who loved him enough to bear it. I could not live with him, and I could not live without him. His mental cruelty became rather like a drug.' She sighed deeply. 'You see he believed his own lies, in the life he had made a charade. Whatever he had planned with you, Miss Clements, he would believe in *at the time,* and no matter how dreadful all this is now, you will have been spared so much suffering – so much suffering.'

Gina's voice was no more than a whisper. 'At first he said he would tell you the truth and ask for a divorce, and then that *you* were a schizophrenic whom, one day, he would have to kill in order to be free. I *believed* him.'

Mrs Wells sat in her chair like something

inanimate. Just a pile of black material. The Inspector looked down at her. 'Your part in all this–'

'I would have killed for her. I've looked after her as though she were my child. My *child*. Can't you see that?'

'Very little escapes me… You hid the murder weapon. And turned suspicion on Miss Selby. Fortunately, we found that weapon – you had not buried it deeply enough, or wiped all the fingerprints off.' He looked back at Vanessa who said pitifully: 'I did not mean to kill him that way. I heard him go downstairs and followed him into the study. He began raving – his temper was a madness and his taunts were more than I could bear. As he came towards me, I picked up that African panga and hit out with it–' She covered her face with her hands. 'The next thing I knew was that I'd killed him. I crept back to bed. It all seemed part of a nightmare. Even now, I can't believe it.'

Mrs Wells cried out, 'He was a brute; a brute.'

Vanessa might not have heard as she said to Carla, '*I* gave Mrs Wells the brooch and letter… I wrote to Paris, too. I thought that if anything happened, you could come to me. I must have been mad… I think it was knowing about the cottage, listening to his lies. Now it is all over. I'm glad; I should have told the truth, anyway, in the end. I'd much rather go with him… He was my child as well as my husband.'

A policewoman had moved into the room. Vanessa saw her in shadow. 'I'll get my coat.'

Mrs Wells got to her feet, the Inspector said curtly, 'You are charged with being an accessory after the fact and for withholding evidence.'

Carla exclaimed, '*You* took my clothes to the cottage.'

'Yes, I took them.' It was almost a hiss. 'I'd have done anything to spare her and now–'

Carla looked at the Inspector. 'May I go upstairs and have a word with–'

He nodded.

Carla reached the landing just in time to see Vanessa rushing into her, Carla's, bedroom, the policeman running after her. She stopped at the door and Carla heard the key turn in the lock. The policewoman cried, 'She moved like the wind.'

'The window,' Carla said in a shriek which brought Adrian and the Inspector up the stairs.

Vanessa stood at the window and looked down on the creek which shimmered in the moonlight. No one could touch her now. The farce, the tragedy, the violence was over. Her heart might have stopped beating already… Perhaps death might be kinder, more gentle, than life…

18

Carla moved to the Fowey Hotel for the few days following Vanessa's death. She felt stunned and incapable of accepting the drama through which she had lived. Her parents had kept in touch with her by telephone, and she blessed them for their sympathy and understanding. She longed to be home, while knowing that, without Adrian, the word sounded hollow and meaningless. And although she had seen him, they had avoided discussing the tragedy. It was too close to be bearable. Locally gossip was rife, but behind it there was no malice. Polvose had become a house of shadows, haunted; its history the subject of speculation.

For all that, Carla was drawn back to it the evening before she left Cornwall. It seemed to have a brooding sadness as though it had absorbed the unhappiness and reflected it uncannily. Until relatives could be traced, it would remain empty. Wells had gone to his brother while his wife was in custody.

Carla walked slowly over the familiar ground – her last tribute to Vanessa whose suffering she was only now beginning to comprehend. Around her the silence was of

Cornwall – as was the incomparable setting. She could not, in the circumstances, mourn for Vanessa, only for the misery she endured. Over it all, the thought of Adrian was heartache and the memories poignant. She told herself that it was folly to allow nostalgia to weaken her. Life lay ahead and she could not escape from it.

The sound of a car coming up the drive gave her the eerie sensation that accompanies the idea of ghosts.

It was *his* car and she hurried towards it.

'I thought I might find you here,' he said.

'Why?'

'Perhaps a little of your woman's intuition brushing off on me.' He shot her a swift glance. 'Saying goodbye to Vanessa?'

'Yes. Going over things, too.' She turned her gaze upon him. 'We haven't talked.'

He nodded agreement. 'Now we can.'

'How much did you know?'

'Everything and nothing, because unless you can fit all the parts of the jigsaw into position, you haven't a picture.'

'You seemed to have a very definite one about me.'

'That makes two of us. Melvin told me in the beginning that Vanessa was the schizo-phrenic. Before I forget, that was what I thought you should know.'

'And then changed your mind.'

'True. I was glad that I did. I learned later

that Melvin had been in a mental home. She protected him all the time. And she lived with fear, even though she did build up her defence in advance. The thing that finished her was his infidelity – but not enough to leave him.' He shot at her, 'Why did you go to the cottage?'

'Because having met Melvin on that cliff walk, I knew he must have some reason for being there. I promised him I would not tell Vanessa that he was in Polvose when he was supposed to be in Paris – without warning him first. But it gave me an advantage in case of any trouble. That was why he bent and kissed my cheek that night.'

'Oh… But you knew Gina.'

'I saw her twice – the second time to tell her to keep away from Polvose.' Carla had to know if Adrian had ever really suspected her of Melvin's murder. She put the question bluntly.

'I was terrified in case you might be in Mrs Wells' position – through loyalty to Vanessa. I suspected her the day you both came to see me at the office. Her concern for your safety was off key. Had she been so concerned, she would have sent you home.'

Carla gasped, 'You mean that you did not really believe Melvin intended to murder her?'

'Just that. It could have happened, but at the back of my mind was the fear that *she* would murder *him.*'

'But – but – she gave her reasons to the Inspector.'

'They were honest reasons, but hurt is rather like rust, it can eat anything away, and she had lived with it for too long. She did not quite realise her own motives. Love and hate can be allies. And while we were all fearing for her, what an alibi should that hate explode.'

Carla shook her head in bewilderment.

'Take the window incident. In the beginning, it was she who intended to push Melvin out of it. He was destroying her: she knew it. I sensed it. No one could fail to do so.' He added gently, 'Don't misunderstand me, I am quite certain that, in given circumstances, she could have killed him because she loved him too much to see him back in a home. She clung to that, if you like, as a justification should she, herself, reach breaking point. She *knew* about Gina and the cottage; about Perth. She did not tell *you* about Gina because, as she said, she needed your help. You were an eye-witness.'

The silence between them froze on the breath of tragedy.

'What she must have gone through – *hell.*'

'He was a sadist; he fed on her misery.'

'But she still loved him. I remember so much that she said.'

'No question about that ... her words that

she could not live with him and could not live without him. Carla, believe me, those were her truest words. It was ironic that she finally killed him unintentionally.'

Carla felt very still, almost weak. 'I am glad she is dead – for her sake.' As she spoke she looked up at the house, the evening sun lay upon it, but the shadows were deep as though etched by centuries. She shivered. And she knew she would never return there.

They got into the car without speaking, and sat staring down the drive. Carla remembered the night when she first arrived there and had heard Melvin (as she now knew) raving. And Vanessa, like a wraith, going down that very same drive. The way she had halted, turned, and gone back...

'I think a drink is what we need,' Adrian said. 'At your hotel?'

'Yes; the view from the cocktail bar is so beautiful.'

'And tomorrow,' Adrian said, as they sipped their martinis, 'you will be back home.'

'Yes.'

He looked at her. 'Why not let me drive you back.'

'You?'

'Don't make me sound like poison.'

'But – why?'

'Because I want to marry you,' he said quietly. 'And now you've tipped most of that drink in your lap.'

'Enough to make anyone–'

'Is that supposed to be an answer?'

'Yes.' She was startled, excited, and happy to the point of disbelief.

'I have always loved you. I never really flirted. I was just hopeful.'

Carla finished wiping her dress.

'I shall need strength to cope with you.'

They smiled at each other – a little intimate smile, that held emotion, passion and tenderness.

'I can't kiss you in front of an audience.'

'Then we'd better go.' Her voice lilted.

'And never part with that dress,' he whispered.

The publishers hope that this book has given you enjoyable reading. Large Print Books are especially designed to be as easy to see and hold as possible. If you wish a complete list of our books please ask at your local library or write directly to:

Dales Large Print Books
Magna House, Long Preston,
Skipton, North Yorkshire.
BD23 4ND

This Large Print Book, for people
who cannot read normal print,
is published under the auspices of

THE ULVERSCROFT FOUNDATION

... we hope you have enjoyed this book.
Please think for a moment about those
who have worse eyesight than you ...
and are unable to even read or enjoy
Large Print without great difficulty.

You can help them by sending a
donation, large or small, to:

**The Ulverscroft Foundation,
1, The Green, Bradgate Road,
Anstey, Leicestershire, LE7 7FU,
England.**
or request a copy of our brochure for
more details.

The Foundation will use all donations
to assist those people who are visually
impaired and need special attention
with medical research, diagnosis
and treatment.

Thank you very much for your help.